## "I like you, Ava Archer."

Heat suddenly rushed to her face, and in an effort to hide it, she turned and grabbed up her tote.

"Don't worry about it, Bowie. It's just a nurse thing. You'll get over it."

He chuckled again. "I wouldn't bet on that either."

Not daring to glance his way, she walked to the door. "Remember to keep your ankle elevated as much as possible. And make sure you don't get your bandages wet."

"I already know all that stuff. Tell me something I don't know."

She glanced over her shoulder to see he was looking at her, and as her gaze slipped over his fresh, rugged face, she realized she felt more alive than she had in years.

A faint smile tugged at her lips even though she was trying to stop it. "I like you, too, Bowie Calhoun."

"Will I see you tomorrow?"

"You'll see me every day until my job here is finished."

A corner of his mouth lifted in a sexy grin. "Then I'll have to make sure your job lasts a long, long time."

And she was going to have to make sure to keep this man at a safe distance, she thought. Otherwise, she was going to forget she was a nurse and remember she was a woman.

**Whether ranchers** ̶ ̶ ̶ ̶ ̶ ̶ ̶ ̶ **rs can ride, shoo** ̶ ̶ ̶ ̶ ̶ ̶ ̶ ̶

Dear Reader,

When the Calhoun brothers first appeared in my mind, I realized Bowie would be the last to find his true love. Being the baby of the bunch, he needed time to grow up and find himself as a man. Now, after years as a marine, he's come home to the family ranch and thinks he knows exactly what he wants in life—freedom and excitement. He certainly isn't dreaming of spending his days chasing cows and his nights with a wife and kids. Until he meets nurse Ava.

Christmas is coming to the Silver Horn Ranch! Will Santa bring Bowie the wife he wants? Or will Bowie need a holiday miracle to convince Ava he's all grown up and ready for marriage?

I hope you'll join me in visiting the Calhouns as they celebrate Christmas. And I wish each of you a blessed holiday of your own.

Merry Christmas!

*Stella Bagwell*

# Christmas on the Silver Horn Ranch

Stella Bagwell

**HARLEQUIN**® SPECIAL EDITION®

Recycling programs
for this product may
not exist in your area.

ISBN-13: 978-0-373-65929-6

Christmas on the Silver Horn Ranch

Copyright © 2015 by Stella Bagwell

**Printed in U.S.A.**

After writing more than eighty books for Harlequin, **Stella Bagwell** still finds it exciting to create new stories and bring her characters to life. She loves all things Western and has been married to her own real cowboy for forty-four years. Living on the south Texas coast, she also enjoys being outdoors and helping her husband care for the horses, cats and dog that call their small ranch home. The couple has one son, who teaches high school mathematics and is also an athletic director. Stella loves hearing from readers. They can contact her at stellabagwell@gmail.com.

### Books by Stella Bagwell

### Harlequin Special Edition

#### Men of the West

*Daddy Wore Spurs*
*The Lawman's Noelle*
*Wearing the Rancher's Ring*
*One Tall, Dusty Cowboy*
*A Daddy for Dillon*
*The Baby Truth*
*The Doctor's Calling*
*His Texas Baby*
*Christmas with the Mustang Man*
*His Medicine Woman*
*Daddy's Double Duty*
*His Texas Wildflower*
*The Deputy's Lost and Found*
*Branded with his Baby*
*Lone Star Daddy*

#### Montana Mavericks: Striking It Rich

*Paging Dr. Right*

#### The Fortunes of Texas

*The Heiress and the Sheriff*

Visit the Author Profile page at Harlequin.com for more titles.

To my dear friend Marie Ferrarella,
who inspires me to keep writing and smiling.

## Chapter One

"No, Dad. She's not here yet and when she does show her face, I'm going to send her packing. I'm sick and tired of being poked and prodded by nurses," Bowie Calhoun barked into the cell phone. "Now that I'm home and away from that damned hospital, I don't want another nurse putting her grubby hands on me!"

"Simmer down, Bowie. Someone has to care for your injuries. Those burns—"

Since his father, Orin, was calling from the horse barn down at the ranch yard, Bowie said the first thing that entered his mind. "Then send Doc Pheeters up here to the house. If he's good enough to deal with Silver Horn horses, he's good enough for me."

Before his father could say more, Bowie ended the call and tossed the cell phone onto a small table next to his armchair. He was being a jerk, but he couldn't help it.

Having second-degree burns on his back and arms was bad enough to endure, but he was also dealing with a broken ankle, which was now held together with screws and encased in a bulky cast.

After being hospitalized for three weeks, getting to come home yesterday had been a great improvement. Still, the idea of being confined to the ranch house for the next few weeks was practically unbearable. Especially to a twenty-six-year-old man loaded with energy. He wanted to get back on the fire line with his buddies. He wanted excitement and fun. He hardly wanted to sit around and watch a herd of cows chew on clumps of buffalo grass.

He bent forward to rearrange his casted foot to a different position on a footstool when a female voice sounded directly behind him.

"Excuse me, but your nurse with the grubby hands has arrived."

Bowie jerked his head around to see a woman in a white nurse's uniform that hugged her tall, curvy figure. He was stunned by the sight. In spite of the frown on her lovely features, Bowie was instantly convinced she was the sexiest woman he'd ever laid eyes on.

Awkward silence filled the room as he searched for the words to help him climb out of the hole he'd dug. "Sorry, I didn't know you were there."

"Obviously."

Bowie had never felt lost in female company. Until this moment. This woman was staring at him as if she wanted to choke him, and he could hardly blame her.

"Well, now that you're here, you might as well shut the door and come on in," he said lamely.

The nurse remained where she stood. "Why should I do that? The vet can tend to you."

Reaching for a crutch propped against the side of the chair, Bowie quickly maneuvered himself to his feet and crossed the parquet floor until he was standing in front of her.

"I'm sorry you had to hear that," he said. "You caught me venting a bit of frustration. It wasn't anything personal toward you."

One black brow arched with skepticism and Bowie couldn't keep his gaze from gliding over her dark brown hair, pale porcelain skin, high cheekbones and full cherry-colored lips. Yet it was her eyes that garnered most of his attention. The color of a clear spring sky, they were almond shaped and framed by incredibly long lashes. Behind the cool blue depths, he could see a wealth of intelligence and maturity—two traits he greatly admired in a woman.

"Not personal? I'm the nurse your father hired, and you clearly stated you don't want me touching you."

Hell's bells, why had she chosen that unfortunate moment to walk through the door, Bowie wondered crossly. And when was he going to learn to keep a rein on his temper? Now he was going to have to do some fast talking or this angel in white was going to walk out and never come back.

"Oh, but I do want you touching me," he blurted, then seeing the line of disapproval on her lips, quickly explained, "I mean, uh, I can hardly take care of myself. And I'm sure you're an excellent nurse—with great hands."

Her nostrils flared and for a moment Bowie thought she was going to reach out and slap him.

"I thought the word was *grubby*, Mr. Calhoun," she said stiffly.

He shot her a helpless grin. "All right, you've made your point. I'll admit it. I'm a rascal. Please forgive me, Ms.—?"

"Ava Archer."

Bowie was relieved to see her expression gradually begin to soften. Maybe there was a glimmer of hope that he hadn't ruined everything with this woman.

He extended his hand to hers. "Nice to meet you, Ava Archer. I'm Bowie Calhoun. Guess you already know that, though," he added sheepishly.

She hesitated a moment before finally placing her hand in his. It felt soft and warm and surprisingly strong. Reluctant to end the contact, Bowie held on.

She said, "Yes, it's clear that you're the patient."

"Well, I'd be pleased if you'd call me Bowie. *Patient* makes me sound like I'm an old man, and I'm far from that."

"I can certainly see that, too. Bowie." She cleared her throat and disengaged her hand from his. "Well, if I'm going to be your nurse, then I think we'd better set some ground rules right off."

That didn't sound to Bowie's liking, but he was hardly in a position to protest. Right now he'd be willing to stand on his head if it would keep this sexy nurse around for a few more minutes.

"You're the nurse. I promise to follow your orders."

"Really?"

"Utterly."

She shot him a dubious look before stepping around him. "If that's the case, Bowie, then take a seat and I'll have a look at you."

He pivoted on the one crutch to see she was opening the drapes on the double windows near his bed. Bright sunlight streamed through the windowpanes. Beyond the glass, a ridge of mountains formed a backdrop to a bustling ranch yard full of cowboys, horses and work vehicles.

"In the chair or on the bed?" he asked.

"The bed."

While he made his way to the king-size bed, she crossed the room and picked up a large tote bag she'd left sitting on the floor by the door.

He asked, "Do you know about my injuries?"

She walked over to the bed and made room on the nightstand for the tote. "I'm aware that you have serious burns and a broken ankle. Dr. Pearson is treating your burns. I have his instructions for your home care. Dr. Stillwell is dealing with your broken ankle, and I've been given his instructions, also. But I'm not aware of the circumstances of how you were injured, if that's your question."

With her standing only a step away from him, the faint scent of her drifted to his nostrils. The fragrance reminded him of the tiny flowers his mother used to grow in the backyard.

"I work on a hotshot crew for the Bureau of Land Management. Out of the field office in Carson City," he said. "We were sent to the Texas Panhandle to help with a canyon fire. High winds brought a burning tree down on me."

She paused in pulling items from the bag to glance over her shoulder at him. "You're lucky to be alive."

"Yeah. Real lucky."

Twisting around, she regarded him for long moments. "Are you being sarcastic?"

Surprised by her question, he said, "Why, no. I thank

God every day that he saw fit to save me from that burning hell. Why do you ask?"

She folded her arms across her breast, but that was hardly enough cover to hide her ample curves from Bowie's eyes. The fitted line of her dress emphasized a waist that would be no larger than the span of his two hands, while her hips flared out in the most enticing way. She was definitely more woman than he'd ever held in his arms. And he couldn't believe she'd walked right into his bedroom and into his life.

"Because I see patients all the time who feel sorry for themselves. That attitude isn't conducive to healing."

He grinned at her. "Believe me, Ava, I'm not a man who goes around carrying a bunch of self-pity. That's not to say I enjoy trying to walk with a crutch."

Her gaze swept over him and for the first time in a long time Bowie felt a tinge of color burn his cheeks. He'd never been a vain man. The time he spent in front of the mirror was no longer than it took to shave off his rusty beard. When women looked at him as though they appreciated his looks, he hardly noticed. But having Nurse Ava eyeing him up and down was a totally different matter.

"No," she said. "I don't expect you do."

"I'd rather be fighting fires."

Turning back to the nightstand, she laid a stack of packaged bandages next to a pair of scissors. "You'll be back on the fire line soon enough. First we have to get you well."

Last evening Bowie had been wondering how he was going to tolerate the next few weeks of being confined to the ranch while waiting for his injuries to heal. When his father had told him he'd hired a nurse, Bowie hadn't been bashful about expressing his views on the subject.

The last thing he needed or wanted was some battle-ax coming into his bedroom and ordering him to take off his clothes. But this vision standing by the head of his bed had definitely made the coming days look a whole lot brighter.

"You know, I just spent three weeks in the hospital, and I only saw one other nurse dressed like you. And she was probably forty years old."

"So that makes her five years older than me," she replied in a no-nonsense way. "Is anything wrong with that?"

Bowie was stunned. He never would've guessed her to be a day past twenty-eight. Not that it mattered. She was gorgeous. And he hoped she was single.

He tilted his head in an effort to get a glimpse of her left hand. From what he could see, there was no ring of any sort on her finger.

"Not at all. I just meant that most nurses wear those colored things that look like pajamas."

"They're called scrubs. And they're comfortable and efficient. I just happen to wear a dress because…I guess it suits me."

"Well, you look a damned sight nicer."

She stepped in front of him and reached for the top button on his shirt. The beat of Bowie's heart shifted into overdrive.

"Let's get one thing straight, Bowie. I'm not here for your visual pleasure or your amusement. I'm here to help you get well. That's all."

"Should I close my eyes?" he asked with a grin. "Or would you like to put a blindfold on me?"

Ava would like to do more than that to this young lothario. She'd like to pick up her bag and give him a swift and final goodbye before she walked out of his room and away from this three-story ranch house. But she was a professional with a job to perform. She couldn't allow any patient to get under her skin. No matter how sexy or charming.

Before she'd arrived on the sprawling Silver Horn Ranch this morning, she'd been aware that she would be treating the youngest of the Calhoun brothers. The only one of them who remained single. Other than the information she'd been given on his medical condition, all she knew were snippets of gossip she'd heard through the hospital grapevine. A few of the younger nurses had described Bowie Calhoun as "dreamy" and "hunky" and "a stud." Ava had never been one to pay much heed to gossip. Most of it was exaggerated hearsay, anyway. But perhaps this was one time she should have listened more closely. At least then she would've been prepared for the sight of her patient.

Bowie Calhoun was six feet of honed muscle dressed in ragged blue jeans and a gray chambray shirt. Square jaw, thin chiseled lips and gold-green eyes shaded by a pair of heavy brows were all framed by exceptionally thick tawny-brown hair that reminded Ava of a shaggy lion. The wayward waves fell recklessly over one eye and down the back of his neck. He was one dangerous-looking male, and everything inside Ava was screaming at her to run until there was a safe distance between them. Like thirty or forty miles.

Steeling herself, she stepped closer and reached for the button in the middle of his shirt. The male scent of his skin and hair drifted to her nostrils and for one crazy moment she thought her hands were actually trembling. But she immediately drew in a deep breath and gathered her senses. She didn't know what was happening to her, but she was determined to put a quick stop to the crazy reaction she was having to this man.

After working all the buttons free, she pushed the shirt off his shoulders and down his arms, all the while carefully keeping her eyes averted from his muscled chest and arms.

"Right now I want you to lie on your stomach and let me take a look at your back," she said, trying to instill as much firmness in her voice as she could. "I assume your bandages were changed yesterday?"

He stretched out on the nearest side of the bed and turned his head so that it was facing in her direction. "They were changed. Right after my sponge bath. Are you going to give me one of those?"

The sly grin on his face caused her to groan silently. "No. You'll have to get someone else to help you with that. But I will clean your burns and apply new bandages."

"Aw, shucks. I thought I was going to be in for a treat this morning."

A treat? She wanted to remind him that she'd just heard him say he was sick and tired of nurses. Why would he consider her ministrations a treat? Surely a young hunk like him didn't find a woman nine years older than him attractive.

*Wrong, Ava. Bowie is the type who'd flirt with a ninety-year-old grandmother if it would be to his advantage.*

Shoving away the mocking voice in her head, she said, "Maybe I can find a lollipop in my tote. All kids deserve a treat after they receive medical attention."

"Hmm. And she has a sense of humor, too. Where have you been all my life?"

During the thirteen years Ava had worked as a nurse, she'd dealt with plenty of flirtatious patients. Leering men with glib tongues came with the job. Mostly, she didn't give their behavior a second thought. But something about Bowie Calhoun was different. Even though she was trying to ignore him, he was getting to her in a way she would've never expected.

"I live in Carson City," she said as casually as she could. "What about you? Is this where you normally live? Or are you here because you need your family's help while you recuperate?"

"My job on the hotshot crew is likely to take me anywhere across the West. Especially during the height of fire season. Otherwise, the Silver Horn is my home. My great-grandfather Calhoun first built the place more than a hundred years ago. Now it's one of the biggest ranches in western Nevada. Is this your first visit to the ranch?"

There was no bragging in his voice, just pride, and Ava liked that about him. Especially when he had plenty to brag about. And suddenly she was very curious about this young man and his place in the wealthy Calhoun family. Mainly, why would he be working at a dangerous job with a modest salary rather than doing something here on the ranch?

She said, "I've been out here a few times before. Two of those visits were when Lilly and Rafe's babies were christened. Each time the christening was followed by a celebration here at the house."

Her answer appeared to surprise him.

"So you're acquainted with my brother and sister-in-law?"

"I've only met Rafe a few times. But I've been friends with Lilly for several years. We worked together when she was still at Tahoe General."

"I see. Did she pick you out for this job?"

"No. Chet Anderson picked me for the job."

"Who's he?"

"Director of nurses at Tahoe General. I'm told he's friends with your father."

"Oh. Well, I should've known. Dad is determined to see that I get the best of care. Are you the best, Ava Archer?"

Now that he was lying prone on the bed, she could see a large bandage on his left shoulder blade, two more protected areas on his left arm and another huge one on the right side of his back just below his rib cage. From her experience with treating burns, she knew that he'd experienced some serious pain.

"You'd have to ask my superiors that question," she replied. "But don't worry, I'll do my best to make this as gentle as possible. Have you been taking your meds?"

"The antibiotics and the vitamins. Not the ones for pain. I prefer to have all my senses about me."

"There's no need for you to try to be a hero." She positioned his arm so that the back was exposed, then reached for the scissors. As she began to cut away the bandages, she tried not to notice the massive width of his shoulders or the bulging muscles in his arms. No doubt the man was as strong as a bull.

*What does that have to do with you changing a patient's bandages, Ava? You're supposed to be focused on Bowie's injuries. Not his masculine charms.*

The return of the annoying voice in her head caused Ava to press her lips to a thin line. She didn't need to be reminded that her thoughts were straying. She'd lost the reins on most of them the first moment she'd laid eyes on him.

Determined to get back to the task at hand, Ava carefully peeled back the special bandage protecting the burn. The mottled flesh was still a long way from regrowing a normal layer of skin. But mercifully there were no signs of infection.

He said, "I've never had ambitions of being a hero."

The tone of his voice was a mixture of rough huskiness and teasing lilt. Each time he spoke the sound sent a tiny wave of pleasure through her.

"What sort of ambitions do you have, Bowie?"

"Excitement. Fun. Living life to the fullest."

His answer was exactly what she'd expected. Even in his battered condition, he possessed a reckless zest for living. And that disappointed her greatly. Why, she didn't know. This young man was just a patient she would be treating for a few weeks and would never see again once the job was finished. What his future held meant nothing to her.

"Sounds like a lofty goal," she finally replied.

He chuckled and Ava decided the sound was even more pleasant than his speaking voice. His laugh reminded her of a time in her life when the whole world seemed bright and beautiful, and life was full of incredible joy.

"I thought so, too," he said. Then, lifting his cheek off the mattress, he attempted to look at her from the corner of his eye. "What sort of ambitions do you have, Ava? Marrying some good-looking guy? Or do you already have a husband?"

None of that was his business. But since she was treating him in such an intimate setting, it would seem ridiculous not to tell him a little about herself. After all, what would it hurt?

"I'm not married. I'm a widow."

Heaven help her, why had she added that? Ava didn't go around announcing she'd been widowed, especially to people she'd just met. It was a fact she'd rather not talk about. But something had suddenly pushed the words from her mouth, as though it was important for this man to understand who and what she was.

"A widow," he repeated thoughtfully. "I'm sorry. Real sorry."

She'd not expected to hear such sincerity in his voice, and the idea that he might genuinely care struck a deep chord in her.

"Thank you. I lost Lawrence thirteen years ago. But that… Well, it's still hard for me, you know."

"To be honest, I can't say that I do know. I've never been married or even engaged, so I can't imagine what it would be like to lose a spouse. Maybe Lilly has told you our father is a widower. After our mother died, I saw him broken with grief. It wasn't anything I'd want to see again."

Her gaze left his arm to settle on the side of his face. The sober expression on his features was quite a contrast to the flirty guy of a few moments ago. Maybe the man wasn't fun and games all the time, she thought.

"Lilly did mention that Mr. Calhoun had lost his wife. But she didn't go into the circumstances," Ava told him. "How long has your mother been gone?"

"Nine years. Those stairs you climbed to get up here to my bedroom—she took a misstep and fell down them.

It caused a blood clot in her head. I had just gone into the Marine Corps when the accident happened."

She stared at him. To hear his mother had died of a tragic accident was one thing, but then he'd dropped another stunner. "You were in the military?" she finally asked.

"Ever since I turned eighteen. It's been close to a year since I left and moved back here from the base in California. After that I went through training for the hotshot crew and went to work fighting wildfires."

So he'd gone from being a soldier to a firefighter. He clearly had no intentions of slowing down just yet. But why would he, she asked herself. He was still young, with no responsibilities other than himself.

"I see."

When she didn't say more, he asked, "What's wrong? You have something against military men?"

Haunting memories suddenly crowded their way into her thoughts, forcing her to swallow before she could utter a word. "No. I don't have anything against the military. It's just that Lawrence was a soldier. In the army. That's how he died—in the Middle East. He was only twenty-five."

Once again he lifted his head from the mattress to look at her. The keen search of his green eyes was so disturbing, she quickly dragged her attention back to his arm.

"Oh. That's rough. I was deployed to Qatar for a while, but never any countries raging with conflict. So I never saw action. Some of my buddies did, though."

She soaked a cotton pad with peroxide and carefully dabbed at the adhesive residue on his healthy skin. "What made you get out of the service? Tired of the restrictions?"

"No matter what sort of job we have, Ava, we all live

with some sort of restrictions. But as for me getting out of the Marines, eight years was enough. I began to get an itch for something new. I started wondering about other possibilities and how I could challenge myself. And my family had been pressing me to come home for a long time. Especially my dad and grandfather. By the time I finished the final year of my stint, I was ready to see Nevada again."

Ava was exchanging too much personal information with this man, she decided. Yes, there were plenty of patients who wanted to talk about their lives and their families. And she always listened, because talking was cathartic for a sick or injured person. But the more this man revealed about himself, the more she was drawn to him. And that was dangerous for her job and her peace of mind.

She reached for a tube of medicated cream and carefully began to spread it over the raw flesh. "Do your other brothers also live here on the Silver Horn? I know that Rafe and Lilly live here in the ranch house and Clancy and his wife have a home on the property."

"Finn got married a few months ago and lives in Northern California now. He and his wife raise horses. And Evan married a woman with a ranch several miles southeast of Carson City. My sister, Sassy, is a ranch woman, too. She and her husband, Jett, have their own ranch northeast of Carson City. Although this past month she's had to slow down much of her ranch work. She gave birth to a baby son about three weeks ago. Little Mason has an older brother and sister, so she has her hands full."

"Your sister must be quite a woman if she helps run a ranch and takes care of three small children, too," Ava said thoughtfully.

"Even with two good feet, I wouldn't be able to keep up with Sassy."

"So all the Calhouns are involved with ranching in some form or fashion. Why aren't you?"

He didn't answer immediately, then finally he said, "Never thought I was that much of a cowboy, I guess."

Ava figured there was much more to his reasoning than that, but she was hardly going to press the issue. She'd already asked him far too much about himself. The last thing she needed was for him to think she was interested in him as a man. Because she wasn't. She cared about his health, but nothing more. She wasn't sure she could ever really care about another man. Not after losing Lawrence.

She removed a second bandage from his arm and carefully medicated the area before covering the two wounds with clean dressings. He remained quiet until she started to work on his shoulder blade.

"Your hands are very gentle. Has anyone ever told you that?"

"I don't remember."

"You're not on a witness stand," he reasoned. "You can answer truthfully without incriminating yourself."

That teasing lilt was back in his voice and Ava decided he must be Irish to the core. "You're not supposed to be asking me such things. And I'm not supposed to be answering."

He chuckled. "Who's going to know what we talk about? I promise my room isn't bugged with a microphone or recorder."

"Look, I don't date—if that's what you're getting at. And frankly, I don't know why any of that would interest you."

"Why wouldn't it interest me?"

Pausing, she studied the back of his head. He had the most beautiful hair. Thick and wavy, the tawny color gleamed like a polished penny. "I'm sure you have a busy life. With plenty of girls to keep you occupied. I'm boring stuff."

"Hmm. You don't look boring to me."

Each time she thought she could shut him up, he came back with something she wasn't expecting. Perhaps if she remained quiet, he'd do the same. But she seriously doubted that would work. He seemed to be enjoying himself too much.

"Are you one of those guys who are attracted to older women?"

"Never thought about it before. You're the first. I mean, the first older woman I've found attractive."

Dear heaven, she was thirty-five. That was hardly ancient. But compared to him she felt like it. He was still very young, with so much in his life to look forward to.

*You have plenty to look forward to, also, Ava. You just don't want to see it. You'd rather stare into the past and wonder how things would've been if Lawrence had lived.*

There it was again. That little spark in her that refused to surrender to reality. If she ever let herself be swayed by it, she'd be in big trouble, Ava thought.

"Thank you for the compliment," she told him. "If that's what it was meant to be. But my life consists of working, eating and sleeping."

"No playing mixed in with all that?"

She kept her gaze fixed firmly on the tortured flesh of his shoulder. Apparently this part of his body had taken the major brunt of the flaming tree. Evidence of contusions spread away from the burned area. The yellow and purple shades told Ava he was healing, but she couldn't help thinking how fortunate he was to be alive. He'd said he was thankful he'd been rescued, yet she wondered if he was actually aware of the extreme danger his life had been in.

"I'm not the playful type," she answered.

Before she could guess his intention, he lifted his head and rolled onto his good shoulder so that he was looking straight at her. "Then we need to do something about that."

There was no mistaking the wicked little grin on his face, and she promptly placed a hand at the back of his head and pushed him back down to the mattress.

"You're in no condition to be doing anything," she said flatly. "Except following doctor's orders."

His chuckle was muffled by the bedcover and for some reason the sound made her wonder what it would be like to be between the sheets with this man and have nothing between them but hot skin. How would it feel to surrender to all that masculine strength and passion?

The fact that she was even imagining such things was enough to jangle her senses. Lawrence was the only man she'd ever made love to, and since she'd lost him Ava had balked at the notion of another man touching her in an intimate way. So why was this man breaking into her safe little world? Why was he making her breath catch and her heart pound? It was crazy and scary and she had to put a quick end to it.

"I won't be in this condition too much longer," he reminded her.

His taunting voice broke into her runaway thoughts, and she resisted the urge to rip a piece of adhesive tape from his healthy skin. "That's right. And once you're healed, you won't ever see me again."

"I wouldn't bet on that."

The teasing tone of his voice had changed to a husky promise, and Ava inwardly shivered. There were all kinds of retorts and reprimands she could shoot back at him. But it was becoming clear that if she jumped into a verbal sparring match with Bowie Calhoun, she'd wind up the loser.

With her lips pressed to a determined line, she silently redressed the remainder of his wounds, then turned back to the nightstand to gather her things.

"Are you finished?" he asked.

*In more ways than one,* Ava thought grimly. "Yes. You may sit up and put your shirt on."

"Aren't you going to help me with it?"

She wanted to bark a loud, clear no. But his arm and shoulder had to hurt. To punish him because of her body's crazy responses was hardly professional. And that was the sole reason she was here at this sprawling ranch—to be this man's nurse.

Sighing, she reached for the gray shirt lying at the foot of the bed and carefully eased it over his left arm and shoulder and then the right. When she finally pulled the fronts together in the middle of his chest, he lifted his head and Ava found herself looking straight into his eyes. The connection caused her heart to take a wild leap.

"I'm sorry if I made you angry," he said gently.

She dropped her gaze from his and focused on buttoning the shirt back together. "I'm not angry."

"Good. Because I like you, Ava Archer."

Heat suddenly rushed to her face, and in an effort to hide it, she turned and grabbed her tote.

"Don't worry about it, Bowie. It's just a nurse thing. You'll get over it."

He chuckled again. "I wouldn't bet on that, either."

Not daring to glance his way, she walked to the door. "Remember to keep your ankle elevated as much as possible. And make sure you don't get your bandages wet."

"I already know all that stuff. Tell me something I don't know."

She glanced over her shoulder at his fresh, rugged face and realized she felt more alive than she had in years.

A faint smile tugged at her lips even though she was trying to stop it. "I like you, too, Bowie Calhoun."

"Will I see you tomorrow?"

"You'll see me every day until my job here is finished."

A corner of his mouth lifted in a sexy grin. "Then I'll have to make sure your job lasts a long, long time."

And she was going to have to make sure to keep this man at a safe distance, she thought as she quickly stepped through the door and shut it firmly behind her. Otherwise, she was going to forget she was a nurse and remember she was a woman.

## Chapter Two

Later that morning, Bowie hobbled his way down the stairs and into the family room at the back of the house. He was surprised to find his sister-in-law Lilly and Tessa, the Calhouns' young house servant, decorating a huge Douglas fir. Colleen, his two-year-old niece, and her eleven-month-old brother, Austin, were both underfoot as they tried to get in on the fun.

"Hey, what's going on here?" Bowie asked as he approached the group. "It looks like someone is getting ready for Santa Claus."

The cheerful boom of his voice had both children forgetting about the tree and racing over to greet their uncle. Colleen immediately grabbed his leg and hung on, while Austin held his arms up and begged for Bowie to hold him.

Lilly called to her young daughter. "Colleen! Don't

grab Uncle Bowie like that! You're going to knock him over!"

Bowie laughed as he looked down at the two young children. Colleen was the blond-haired, blue-eyed image of her mother, while little Austin favored the Calhouns with his strawberry-colored curls and green eyes. It still amazed Bowie that Rafe had been the first one of his brothers to have children. Rafe had always been such a playboy. But falling in love with Lilly had definitely changed his rowdy ways. Now his brother was more than content to spend his free time with his wife and babies. Bowie adored women, and he liked children, too, but he couldn't imagine making them the center of his life.

"If little Colleen can knock me over, then I'm ready for the nursing home." Using his good arm, he scooped up Austin and gathered the boy to the right side of his chest. The effort caused him a bit of discomfort, but he hid it carefully. Showing any sign of weakness wasn't his style. Which made his injuries that much harder to bear.

He said, "Come on, kids, let's go have a look at this Christmas tree."

Lilly shook her head at Bowie. "You shouldn't be carrying Austin. In fact, you shouldn't have come down the stairs without me or Tessa helping you," she scolded. "Why didn't you call for one of us? And you're only using one crutch!"

"I was careful. And two crutches are cumbersome. One works better," he told her. "So what's with the tree? Isn't it early to be decorating for Christmas?"

She shot him a playful frown. "This isn't a marine barracks, Bowie. And it's the second of December. It's time to start decorating. Haven't you looked outside?

Dad has some of the hands putting up the lights on the house and in the yard."

This would be Bowie's first Christmas since his return home from the Marines. During the years of his military service, he'd managed to get furlough and spend a few holidays here at the ranch, but that wasn't the same as living here. He'd almost forgotten all the hoopla that took place on the ranch prior to Christmas. The kitchen was always full of rich food and every room was decorated in some form or fashion. Even the barns were strung with lights and the horse stalls adorned with wreaths and bows.

"I haven't noticed," Bowie told her. "The nurse was here to change my bandages. I'm still trying to recover from her visit."

Surprised by his news, Lilly said, "Oh, I wasn't aware Ava was starting the job today. I would've come up and said hi to her. Uh, why are you still trying to recover? Was it that painful?"

"It wasn't painful at all. I was only teasing." But Ava's visit had been eye-opening, Bowie could have told his sister-in-law. He still couldn't shake her image from his mind, much less the sound of her voice or the tender touch of her hands. He'd been around plenty of women in his life, but none of them came close to affecting him the way she had. "She got me all fixed up. No problem."

"Great. When Dad said Chet was sending Ava out to nurse you, I knew she'd be perfect."

"She told me you two are friends," Bowie commented.

Lilly nodded. "We've been friends and coworkers for several years. Although now that I work at the clinic, I don't get to see her very often."

There were lots of things Bowie would have liked to

ask Lilly about her friend, but he wasn't going to. He didn't much care for snooping into a person's private life. He preferred to ask the person face-to-face. And he'd already found out much more about the nurse during her short visit than he'd expected to. The fact that she was a widow, and had remained single for all these years, was still nagging at him.

"Well, well, little brother has come down to join the land of the living."

Rafe's voice had Bowie glancing over his shoulder to see his older brother walking into the room. He was dressed in batwing chaps and a sheepskin-lined coat. A soiled felt Stetson was pulled low on his forehead, while spurs jangled on his boot heels. Rafe wasn't just the image of a cowboy, Bowie thought, he was a cowboy inside and out. As foreman of the Silver Horn, his brother had the enormous job of keeping a crew of men working and a few thousand head of cattle healthy and producing.

"I'm already pretty damned bored with that bedroom," Bowie told him.

"The last time I looked, you had a TV, a stack of movies, books, a stereo and a laptop in your room. That isn't enough toys to keep you occupied?" Rafe teased.

"You're making me sound spoiled, when all I want is a little human company. By the way, what are you doing in the house at this hour?"

"Greta promised to make cookies for the fence crew. They're working out on Antelope Range, replacing barbed wire on some of the cross fencing. And since it's starting to snow, I thought I'd drive out and give the boys an early treat of hot coffee and cookies. Want to come along?"

"To Antelope Range? If I remember right, that's several miles out there," Bowie said.

Rafe chuckled. "Well, if you need to stay where you'll be warm and cozy, then go ahead."

"Rafe!" Lilly protested. "Bowie hasn't been out of the hospital even two days yet. He needs to recuperate before you start dragging him all over creation."

Just hearing Rafe accuse him of being soft was enough to make Bowie set little Austin on the floor and turn toward his brother. "I haven't lost anything out on Antelope Range, but I'll go with you. Otherwise, I'll never hear the end of it."

"Bowie, as a nurse I'm advising you not to leave the house," Lilly insisted.

Rafe cast his wife a subtle look. One that Bowie didn't understand, but Lilly seemed to catch instantly.

"Don't worry, honey," Rafe said. "I won't let him out of the truck. He's only going along for the ride."

Lilly gave her husband a dismissive wave before she turned her attention back to the tree decorations. "I don't like the idea at all. But I can't fight two men at once. And maybe a bit of fresh air will do him good," she reluctantly added.

"Tessa, would you go upstairs and get one of Bowie's old coats and a hat?" Rafe asked the maid. "We'll meet you in the kitchen."

"I'll be right down with them, Rafe," she replied.

Tessa left to fetch the garments, and Rafe and Bowie started out of the room. As they made their way down a hallway, Rafe slowed his stride to match Bowie's hindered pace.

"Look, Rafe, I know you're trying to give me a break, and I appreciate it," Bowie said. "But there's no need for you to waste time on me. When cabin fever starts driving me crazy, I'll go outside and walk around."

"Shut up. This isn't a pity invitation. And if I know you, cabin fever is already driving you crazy. On the way out to Antelope Range, you're going to help me check over a herd of heifers. I want to see if you still have the eye."

"What sort of eye?" Bowie asked as they neared the kitchen.

Rafe chuckled. "A rancher's eye. What else?"

*Yeah, what else?* Bowie thought glumly. But he'd never been a rancher. Not like his brothers. Oh, he knew the workings of a cow and he could ride a horse, but he'd never had the natural instinct that Rafe or Finn had, or his two oldest brothers, Clancy and Evan. Yet that hadn't stopped the members of his family from trying to draw him into the business. On one hand, the idea that they wanted him living and working close to them was endearing. But there was another part of Bowie that none of his brothers or dad or grandfather understood—he needed to be free of constraints. Even those that involved his family. He wanted to do his own thing. Be his own man. Not follow in his family's footsteps.

"Like I said, you're wasting your time," Bowie replied.

"I'll be the judge of that."

In the kitchen Greta, a plump woman in her early sixties, packed the bagged cookies and a large thermos of coffee into a cardboard box and handed it all to Rafe.

"That should keep everything from rolling around on the floorboard of the truck," the cook told him. She cast a skeptical glance at Bowie. "You taking this whippersnapper with you?"

"I thought I could put up with him for a little while," Rafe told Greta.

"Well, don't shake up little Bowie too much. He's in a weakened condition."

Little Bowie. He was six feet tall and weighed a solid one hundred and ninety pounds. He could hardly be described as *little*. But Greta had been cooking for the family since before Bowie was born. To her, he would always be the last son born to Orin and Claudia.

Bowie let out a good-natured groan. "For pity's sake, I'm not a helpless invalid!"

Rafe grinned at his brother. "Don't worry about him, Greta. I hear he's going to have a pretty nurse to keep him healthy."

Greta rolled her eyes. "Yeah, and remember what happened to you the last time a pretty nurse came to the house?"

Laughing, Rafe said, "Sure I remember. She got Grandfather back on his feet and acting like a young man again."

"Ha! She also turned you into a husband and a daddy!"

"What can I say?" Rafe said happily. "I know a good thing when I see it."

Tessa chose that moment to enter the kitchen carrying a green plaid ranch coat and a brown felt cowboy hat.

After propping his crutch against a cabinet, Bowie balanced his weight on his good foot and allowed the young woman to help him pull on the coat.

"It's hell to be helpless," Bowie muttered as he jammed the hat onto his head.

"It's a lot better than being under that burning tree," Tessa said pointedly.

Because Tessa was normally as quiet as a church mouse, both Rafe and Greta burst out laughing.

"Guess she told you," Rafe teased.

"Amen, Tessa," Greta told the maid. "The scamp needs to be reminded how lucky he is."

Bowie started toward the door. "Let's get out of here. I've had all the women I can take for one morning."

Thankfully, Rafe had parked his truck not far from the back door of the kitchen, and Bowie crossed the distance without too much effort.

Once the two men were buckled inside the warm cab and headed in a westerly direction through the ranch yard, Rafe said, "You know, Tessa is pretty fond of you. I hope you'll watch what you say to her. She's got a pretty soft heart."

Bowie shot a look of disbelief at his brother. "Excuse me, but aren't you the same guy who went for years never worrying about breaking a girl's heart?"

Rafe frowned. "I've mended my ways since then."

"Well, Tessa is like a little sister to me. What is she now? Twenty, maybe?"

"She just turned twenty-one."

And she was wasting her young life here on this ranch, Bowie thought. She needed to be in the city with other young people, doing fun and exciting things. But he kept his opinion to himself. Rafe wouldn't understand. He believed there was no place on earth like the Silver Horn. He didn't understand Bowie's need to experience a broader life.

He looked out the passenger window and released a long breath. "Don't worry. I'll be kind to Tessa."

The truck rolled by the big main horse barn and Bowie instantly thought of Finn. Their brother lived in Northern California now with his wife, Mariah, and son, Harry. In a few months, their second child was due to arrive.

"I miss Finn," Bowie said. "When I look at the horse

barn, I still expect him to be there, taking care of the horses. The ranch isn't the same without him around."

"No. But Dad and Colley are doing a good job keeping everything going smoothly with the horses. And let's face it, Finn is finally doing what he's always wanted to do, working with mustangs. I'm happy for him." He glanced over at Bowie. "Now that I think of it, while you're off work recuperating, you ought to go up and spend some time with him and Mariah. They'd be happy to have you."

The idea was appealing. At least then he wouldn't have to listen to his dad or grandfather telling him he needed to strap on his chaps and spurs and get back to being a cowboy. Not that he'd ever been one, Bowie thought dourly. His being a ranch hand was their delusion, not his.

"Can't leave now. I have to have these blasted bandages changed every day for the next few weeks. Maybe longer."

"Oh. Forgot about that. Lilly said the nurse Dad hired is a friend of hers. Have you met her yet?"

Met her? That was hardly the way he would describe the exchange he'd had with the beautiful Ava Archer, Bowie thought.

"She's already been here this morning and left," Bowie said as he stared out the passenger window.

"And?"

Rafe's persistence put a frown on Bowie's face. "She treated my burns and applied clean bandages. That's all there was to it."

Rafe was silent for a moment, and then he burst out laughing.

Bowie cut a sharp glance at him. "You find something funny about that? Maybe you'd like to change places with me?"

His voice still full of humor, Rafe said, "I don't think Lilly would like that too much. In fact, I think she'd put on her nurse's cap and take care of me herself."

When the family learned Bowie was being released from the hospital and would need home care, Lilly had immediately volunteered for the job. Bowie had thanked her for the offer, but he'd not wanted to put his sister-in-law in the awkward situation of seeing him half-naked every day. So Ava had been hired instead. Lovely Ava, who'd lost her husband so long ago.

Bowie remained silent with his thoughts, and Rafe chuckled again.

"So a beautiful woman walks into your bedroom this morning and you have nothing to say about it? You are more than wounded, little brother, you're sick with a fever or something."

Bowie let out a heavy breath. He couldn't hide from Rafe. The two brothers were too much alike.

"Okay, I'll fess up. I got off to a really bad start with Ava," Bowie muttered. "When she walked in I was on the phone telling Dad how I didn't want a nurse. And a few other derogatory things that I wouldn't have wanted any woman to hear. I had to do some fast apologizing to get her to stay."

"Well, Ava's too old for you, anyway. And from what Lilly says, she isn't interested in having a man in her life. Which is unfortunate, if you ask me. The few times I've been around her, she seems like a woman who needs a family."

Why had Rafe had to go and say that kind of thing and ruin the fantasies he'd been having of the sexy nurse? To Bowie, she'd seemed like a woman who needed a man to make love to her.

"Don't look at me. I'm hardly in the market for a wife and kids. Besides, I like younger women. The kind that wants to have fun. Not babies."

"So you're still on that kick. I was thinking now that you've gotten out of the Marines you might be feeling different about women—and other things."

"I might be out of the Marines, but I'm hardly ready for slippers and a recliner every night."

"You're hardly ready for a barroom brawl, either," Rafe said drily. "Have your doctors given you an idea as to when you might go back to work?"

"Barring no complications, in six to eight weeks."

"That quick?"

Bowie groaned. "You call sitting around on this ranch for the next six weeks quick?"

Rafe whipped the truck around a patch of sagebrush growing in the middle of the rough pasture road. "Be patient, Bowie, and you might get to liking it."

So this was why his brother had taken him on this jaunt this morning, Bowie thought. Not for a breath of fresh air or a change in scenery. But to give him a pep talk about giving up the hotshot crew and becoming a full-time rancher.

"Look, Rafe, it's nice that you and the rest of the family want me around. I appreciate that. But this kind of life isn't for me. I'd go out of my mind with boredom. It's one of the reasons I went into the Marines in the first place."

Rafe snorted. "Bull. You didn't go into the Marines because you were bored. You did it because you were a rebel. Hell, Mom was the only one who thought the military would be good for you. And I guess in some ways she was right," he added thoughtfully.

"Mom," Bowie repeated softly. "I sure wish she was

still with us. You know, while I was in the Corps, I often caught myself imagining she was still here on the ranch. But now that I'm home, everything I look at reminds me she's gone."

Rafe glanced his way. "You know, the first time I met Ava, she sort of reminded me of Mom. She's tall and dark and elegant like Mom was. Maybe that's why I connect Ava with having a family. It's just too bad that she can't get past losing her husband."

She didn't want to get past losing him, Bowie thought. But that was her choice and had nothing to do with him. For the next few weeks he was going to enjoy her visits, but beyond that, she was off-limits.

They rounded a rolling hill covered in scraggly juniper, and a small herd of cattle came into view. Bowie was relieved to see them. He didn't want to talk about Ava or hear his brother talking about the woman needing a husband anymore.

"There's a herd off to the right," Bowie said. "Are they the heifers you wanted to look at?"

"Sure are."

Slowing the truck, Rafe steered off the narrow road and toward the black cattle. As soon as the animals spotted the vehicle, they came running with hopes of getting fed.

"If you don't have some feed in the back of the truck," Bowie commented, "those heifers are going to be mighty upset."

Rafe chuckled. "This isn't my first rodeo. I loaded some hay bales earlier."

He parked the truck on a flat space of ground and waited for the cattle to gather nearby. By now fat flakes of snow were splattering against the windshield and dusting the backs of the black cattle. It had been years since Bowie had seen snow and experienced cold weather. He'd almost forgotten the hardship it placed on the livestock and the men who cared for them.

After Rafe had tossed blocks of hay to the cattle, he climbed back into the warm cab and held his gloved hands toward the vents on the dashboard.

"Sorry I can't help," Bowie told him. "I might not be much of a rancher, but I do know how to spread hay."

"You know how to do more than spread hay," Rafe said. "Remember when we were kids and we found that cow down by the river? She was trying to calve and was in really bad shape."

"Yeah. I remember. I argued with you that there wasn't enough time to go back to the ranch and get help. We pulled the calf ourselves."

"And everything turned out good," Rafe said with a wry grin. "I was fifteen and you were only ten. But you had more guts than I did, little brother. If you hadn't been there with me, I would have lit out for the ranch."

"Dad didn't call it guts. He called it being reckless," Bowie reminded him.

"Yeah, but he was happy." He pointed to the heifers. "How do they look to you?"

"Good. Except for those two standing over at the edge. They're not eating and their ears are drooped. They look a little sick to me."

Grinning, Rafe was about to reach over and slap Bowie's shoulder when he suddenly remembered his injuries and pulled back his hand. "Just what I expected. You haven't forgotten a thing about being a cowboy. Welcome home, Bowie."

Bowie started to remind him that he was only going

to be home for a few weeks, but the smile on Rafe's face was such a happy one, he just didn't have the heart to ruin the moment.

Rafe, and everyone else in the family, would learn soon enough that he was heading back to the hotshot crew just as soon as his body had returned to working order.

Ava was still working the emergency room at Tahoe General when her friend and fellow nurse, Paige Winters, entered the sheeted cubicle where Ava was adjusting an IV on an elderly female patient suffering with flu symptoms.

"Are you nearly finished here?" Paige asked.

Ava glanced around at the redheaded nurse dressed in navy-blue scrubs. She was a tall, slender woman with a face dominated by a pair of clear gray eyes. Normally there was a perpetual smile on her face, but at the moment her lips were pressed together in a frustrated line.

"Yes, this patient is being admitted. Why? You need help with something?"

Paige jerked her thumb toward the opposite end of the room. "An unruly male. He slipped on an icy sidewalk and cut his head. He thinks he's dying and demands the doctor see him this instant."

"Dr. Sherman is busy with a cardiac incident right now. And Dr. Garza is tending to a toddler with whooping cough. The patient will just have to wait his turn."

"I wish you'd tell him that."

"You can't?" Ava asked her.

Paige cast her a pleading smile. "I'm not nearly as good with a naughty man as you are."

That was because she didn't think of them as men. She thought of them as people. Except for the one she'd met this morning, Ava thought. Bowie was so potent she'd not been able to think of him as anything but a tough hunk of man.

"All right. I'll deal with him."

After hanging the patient's chart on the end of the bed, Ava left the cubicle with Paige following close on her heels. When the two of them entered the compartment with the head injury, she found a young man sitting on the side of the narrow examining table holding a huge cotton pad to the side of his head. He was dressed in a sports jacket and tie. The knot at his throat was askew and blood splattered the toes of his wing tips.

"What the hell kind of place is this anyway?" he yelled the moment Ava stepped up to him. "I'm bleeding all over the place and nobody cares!"

Ava glanced over to see Paige rolling her eyes.

"Other than taking his vitals, Mr. Dobson here refused to let me touch him," Paige explained. "He'd rather keep bleeding."

"I came here to have my head treated by a doctor!" he practically shouted. "If I'd wanted a nurse to take care of me I'd have driven over to my grandma's house."

"Is your grandma a nurse?" Paige asked.

"No. But she'd know a damned sight more than you two. All I've seen you two do is carry clipboards around in circles."

"See," Paige said to Ava. "He's a real sweetheart."

Ava gave him a wide, phony smile. "This is an emergency room, Mr. Dobson. The most critical patients come first. If you don't want to wait your turn to see the doctor, then perhaps you'd better let your grandma take care of you. Just try not to bleed all over the floor as you leave.

I don't want any of the nurses slipping and falling because of you."

While the man spluttered with outrage, Ava urged her coworker out of the cubicle. "I hope you wrote intoxicated on his chart," she said under her breath.

Paige frowned. "I didn't notice alcohol. But now that you mention it, his eyes are pretty glassy. You don't think that's a result of banging his head?"

"Trust me. He's belted back a few. And he isn't going anywhere. He's too much of a wimp."

"Okay. You've been a nurse a lot longer than me. I'll make a notation on his chart. Thanks, Ava." She glanced at her wristwatch. "I need to go check on another patient. I'll see you in the locker room in thirty minutes."

Ava looked at her with surprise. "Thirty minutes? Is it time for the shift change already?"

Paige grinned. "Time flies when you're having fun."

The past nine hours of Ava's evening shift in the ER had passed in a blur. The half hour she'd spent in Bowie's bedroom this morning had felt like a whole day and then some. Maybe if she'd gone at the job of treating the firefighter like any other patient, the time with him would've spun by. But Bowie Calhoun wasn't just any other patient. He was not like any man she'd met before.

A half hour later, in the nurses' locker room, the two women were changing into street clothes.

"So you want to go get a drink or something to eat?" Paige asked as she slipped on a heavy coat. "I'm starving."

Sitting on a wooden bench, Ava pulled a pair of knee-high boots over her jeans. "Not tonight. It will be one o'clock before I get home and climb into bed. And I need to be out at the Silver Horn by ten."

"Oh. I'd forgotten about you taking on that extra job." The redhead wrapped a long knit scarf around her neck. "Have you taken a look outside? It's been snowing for the past two hours. You might not be able to drive out to the ranch in the morning."

That might be a relief, Ava thought. Or would it? If she didn't see Bowie in the morning, she'd think about him for the rest of the day. On the other hand, everything might be different in the morning, she thought hopefully. She might take one look at the hunky ex-marine and not feel anything at all, except the need to care for a patient.

"If the highways are treacherous, then I'm to call and someone from the ranch will come pick me up in a four-wheel-drive vehicle and drive me out there."

Paige reached for her purse. "You're kidding me."

Ava stood and shrugged on her coat. "No kidding. One way or the other, the family is going to make sure Bowie has his nurse."

"Hmm. Well, I shouldn't be surprised. From what I've heard, the Calhouns have more money than they know what to do with."

Ava pulled the pins from her heavy bun and quickly ran a brush through the long tresses. "I never realized that raising cattle could make a family so wealthy."

"It's more than cattle, Ava. They sell high-priced cutting and show horses, too. And I hear they have lots of other holdings in mining and the gas and oil business."

Ava put away the brush and pulled on her gloves while the image of Bowie lying on the king-size bed flashed into her mind. Surprisingly, he'd not come across to her as rich or spoiled. In fact, he'd seemed very down-to-earth.

But then, she'd only been there for a half hour. A woman would need weeks, even months to learn the sort of man who lived behind that rugged face and muscled body.

"I wasn't aware you knew that much about the family," Ava replied.

"I don't. But I read things in the paper from time to time. And I remember a few years ago, when old Mr. Calhoun was hospitalized. Some of the nurses were hoping he'd have a longer stay just so they'd get to look at the gorgeous grandsons coming to visit. So which one of them are you treating?"

"The youngest. Bowie. He's the only one of them that's still single." Now, why had she bothered to give Paige that piece of information? His marital status had nothing to do with her job.

Paige chuckled slyly. "Lucky for you."

Ava forced herself to laugh along with her friend. She might as well. The idea of her and Bowie ever having a relationship of any sort was totally laughable.

Picking up her handbag, she started out of the small locker room. "Sure," she joked. "Everyone knows what a cougar I am."

## Chapter Three

The next morning the sun was out, but there was a layer of snow covering the patch of yard in front of Ava's house. Snowplows had already cleared the few side streets she took to reach the main highway, but the last ten miles of graveled road leading to the ranch were another story. After a few incidents of sliding and spinning, she managed to reach the Silver Horn, although the effort left her tense and exhausted.

When she eventually entered the house, Greta instantly began to scold her. "Miss Archer, you should have called the ranch for a ride. The roads are messy today."

Ava handed her coat and gloves to Tessa, who was kindly waiting to take her things. "They weren't that bad in town," she told the cook. "But I must say the rural road leading up here to the ranch was treacherous."

Greta clucked her tongue with disapproval. "From now

on, you call and let us know you need a lift. We don't want you hurt, too."

"I'll do that," Ava promised, then asked, "Is Bowie in his room?"

Greta let out a loud, frustrated groan. "He's up there. After he ate his breakfast, he insisted he was going to get in the shower. I told him he couldn't."

"That's right. Only a sponge bath. He can't get his burns or cast wet."

"Well, he won't let me or Tessa help him with a sponge bath. And seeing he was so hell-bent on getting into that shower, I unscrewed the showerhead and brought it down here. He won't be using it for a while. But he's probably still fuming."

Ava had to laugh. "Good thinking. And I'll remind him of what he's to do and not to do."

"Well, brace yourself. He wasn't too happy when I left him," Greta warned.

She was going to brace herself, Ava thought a few minutes later as she climbed the two flights of stairs to Bowie's bedroom. Not because of his present mood, but because she needed to control herself.

After a firm knock, she stepped into the bedroom to see Bowie standing with the aid of his crutch, staring out the window. The brooding expression on his face was a far cry from the playful guy she'd met yesterday.

"Good morning," she said.

His head jerked in her direction as though he'd been expecting anyone but her.

"Oh. I thought it was that damned Greta back to torment me."

Ava shut the door and moved deeper into the room. "It's a good thing the cook is keeping an eye on you. She told me about the shower. Are you trying to ruin everything the doctors have done so far? Maybe you'd like to go through a series of skin grafts. Think a shower would be worth that?"

"Damn it, I just want to feel clean. I can wash the bottom half of me okay. But I can't handle the top half."

"Greta says she and Tessa have offered to help you."

He mouthed another curse under his breath. "Not on your life. Greta is like a grandmother. And Tessa came to live with us when she was just a very young teenager. She's like a baby sister to me. Understand?"

Unfortunately, she did.

Dropping her tote bag on the foot of the bed, she motioned toward the private bathroom. "Okay. I told you yesterday I wasn't going to do this, but I will. Just because I don't want you to have a setback and cause me to have to see you for the next four months instead of the next six weeks."

His eyes widened. "What are you going to do?"

The surprised look on his face was comical. "I'm going to give you a bath. What else?"

"In the bathroom?"

She shook her head in disbelief. "I don't see any soap and water out here. Do you?"

For a moment she thought he was going to start singing a different tune about wanting a bath, but then he heaved out a heavy breath and hobbled off toward the bathroom. Ava followed behind him.

Bowie's private bathroom was nearly as big as her kitchen. A green marble tub was situated on one side, while a glass-enclosed shower spanned the opposite wall. Green and white tile covered the floor, while white towels and washcloths hung on racks conveniently positioned around the room.

Spotting a padded dressing bench over by the tub, she dragged it over to the sink. "Sit down here," she ordered.

"Ava, I—"

"You what? Have decided you don't want a bath as much as you thought you did?"

"No. I still want a bath. I just— Well, it suddenly occurred to me that I probably sound like a spoiled brat to you. And I'm not. I'm just sick of being helpless, that's all."

"And a little bit stubborn to go with it?" she added impishly.

He grinned at that, and Ava was relieved to see his mood lift. She was a nurse—she didn't want him to be miserable. Not physically or mentally.

"Just a little," he admitted.

Turning slightly away from him, she filled the sink with warm water, then gathered a bar of soap and a washcloth. "How did you get that sweatshirt on?"

"Very carefully," he answered. "It hurt my shoulder a bit when I pulled it over my head. But I don't think it damaged anything."

"You don't, do you? Well, let's hope it didn't tear any flesh." She turned back to him. "I can see you're going to be a difficult patient. Didn't you learn to follow rules in the Marines?"

"Yes. And I followed them. But I didn't always like them."

"I see. So now you want to make up your own rules."

"Life is more fun that way."

"You say that word a lot, you know." Stepping closer, she reached for the hem of his sweatshirt. "Bend your head and I'll try to get this thing off. And then I never want to see it again."

After some slow, careful maneuvering, she worked the sweatshirt over his head and tossed the garment aside.

"What word do I say a lot?" he asked.

Deliberately ignoring the sight of his naked chest, she began to soap the wet washcloth. "Fun. That's the word."

"What's the matter? You object to having fun?"

"No. But everything isn't fun and games." She wrung out the cloth and turned back to him. "Now don't move. Otherwise, I'll get soap and water where it doesn't belong."

"I'll be as still as a statue," he promised.

Stepping closer, she decided to start with his good arm and save the more problematic areas for last.

Wrapping her hand around his wrist, Ava held his arm out straight and washed the corded muscles. As she worked, the erotic male scent of his skin and the faint caress of his warm breath against her arm were impossible to ignore. Over the years, she'd done this very same thing to hundreds of male patients. None had made her so aware of being a woman. None had made her feel as though she was touching a man for the very first time.

"I didn't think you'd show up today," he said. "There's quite a bit of snow on the ground."

Ava wasn't going to explain how his father had made plans beforehand to make sure she got to the ranch. From what she could see, Bowie wasn't the sort that appreciated being coddled by his family.

"The drive took a bit longer," she admitted. "But I made it without any problems."

"When the weather is bad, you should stay out here

on the ranch instead of driving back and forth to Carson City. We have plenty of empty rooms."

His invitation took her by surprise. Mainly because she wasn't a friend or even an acquaintance. She was hired help.

"Thank you for offering, but I couldn't do that. I work six nights a week in the ER at Tahoe General."

Finished with his arm, she rinsed the washcloth and started on his shoulder. It was thick and padded with heavy muscle. Even through the thickness of the wet cloth, she could feel the sinewy curves beneath her fingers. The sensation caused her breathing to slow and her hand to linger.

He looked up at her and Ava's gaze dropped to his lips. What would it feel like, she wondered, to have those lips skimming over her skin, to be kissing her mouth until she couldn't breathe?

"No one told me that. I thought you worked freelance or something. Six nights a week. That's a grind, isn't it?"

No, it was a relief, she thought. Working that many nights gave her a reprieve from an empty house and a lonely bed. But she wasn't about to admit such a thing to him. Not for anything did she want this man to pity her. She was living the life she'd chosen. And it was all she wanted or needed.

"Not really. I love my work. I've been a nurse since I was twenty-two—a long time. And it's rewarding to help people. Especially those too sick or injured to take care of themselves."

"Like me?" he asked with a grin.

In spite of her chaotic senses, she managed to give him a faint smile. "You're injured, but not helpless. You just want me to think you are."

"And why shouldn't I? You're a beautiful woman, Ava. And you have hands like an angel."

Ava couldn't remember the last time her heart had raced like a stock car, but it was definitely breaking the speed limit right now.

"Like I said before, I'm not here for your amusement."

"That doesn't stop me from looking and feeling," he said huskily.

By now Ava had forgotten what she was supposed to be doing, until the heat of his skin began to burn through the washcloth. Heaving out a heavy breath, she tossed it into the sink, then tried her best to glare at him. But she simply couldn't come up with enough anger to pull it off.

"Bowie, have you forgotten everything I told you yesterday? I'm thirty-five years old. Doesn't that mean anything to you?"

His green gaze traveled lazily over her face and down the vee of her dress. The intimate search caused Ava's cheeks to burn.

"Sure," he replied. "It means you've had time to grow wiser. And more beautiful. And more womanly."

Those were hardly the answers she'd expected to come out of his mouth, and for a moment she didn't know how to respond. Finally, she asked, "Did the nurses in the hospital have this much trouble with you?"

Although a grin tilted one corner of his lips, there was a serious look in his eye. It bothered Ava far more than all the words he'd said to her.

"The nurses in the hospital weren't you," he said simply.

Struggling with the effort to keep from groaning out loud, Ava grabbed the washcloth and scrubbed the bar of soap against the terry fabric until lather was spilling over her hands.

When she turned back to him, she lifted his head until it was out of the way, then plopped the cloth against his chest. Bubbles and water meshed with the golden-red hair matted between two flat brown nipples. Ava pushed the washcloth up, down and across until his skin was slick.

Over and over, she kept reminding herself that she was only doing her job. Yet nothing about it felt like a job. Touching him this way was taking her on an erotic journey, unlike anywhere she'd ever traveled before.

By the time she reached his navel, she heard him draw in a sharp breath. The sound caused Ava to lift her head. Which was a big mistake. The movement had brought her lips a scant inch away from his.

Her gaze fluttered up to his and suddenly she realized if she didn't take a quick step backward, she was going to be in trouble. But the warning bells clanging in her head weren't enough to make her legs move.

"Am I hurting you?"

The question came out as a whisper and Ava wished she'd not said anything. At least that way he might not have guessed how deeply his nearness was affecting her.

"I'm hurting like hell to do this," he murmured.

Before she could ask what *this* was, his hand was at the back of her head and the next thing she knew her lips were being captured by his.

Stunned by the contact, she started to pull back. But after a split second, she recognized that resisting was the last thing she wanted to do. He tasted like a hot summer night. Like tangled sheets and endless passion. And she wanted his kiss. Desperately.

Her lips yielded to his, then quickly began a search of

their own. How long she stood there, her head bent down
to his, their mouths fused together, she didn't know. She
wasn't sure about anything until the hand at the back
of her head finally fell away and cool space separated
their faces.

Sanity suddenly rushed in to replace her foggy senses,
and she glanced down to see the washcloth she'd been
holding had slipped to his lap. Soapy water had soaked
the front of his jeans and a dark stain spread out from
the fly. "Oh! Damn it! Now look what I've done! What
you've done!"

She whirled her back to him and dropped the washcloth into the sink as if it were aflame. As she sagged
against the vanity counter, Bowie stared at her as he tried
to digest what had just happened. Kissing Ava had set off
a series of explosions in his head, blasts that had been
so strong the aftershocks were still ricocheting through
his body.

"This isn't going to work, Bowie," she said in a low,
firm voice. "I'm going to tell your father he has to find
a different nurse for you."

"No!"

Before he could stop himself, Bowie reached out and
snatched her arm. The contact had her twisting back to
face him.

"What do you mean, no? You don't have a say in this.
Not now! I can deal with your flirting, but kissing me
crossed the line!"

"What about *you* kissing me? That wasn't exactly a
one-sided deal, you know."

His remark must have hit the mark, because her lips

suddenly formed a small O and the rigid line of her shoulders drooped.

"You're right, Bowie. I was kissing you, too. Which gives me two reasons why I can't remain your nurse."

Just hearing her say she was leaving and not coming back was enough to shake Bowie. "Ava, I'm sorry."

Her expression sober, she studied his face. "I'm sure. You must be feeling like an idiot for letting yourself kiss an older woman."

"I'm not sorry about that! I'm not sorry about anything I've done!"

"You just said you were," she reminded him.

"That because I thought it was what you wanted to hear," he admitted.

With an exasperated groan, she started to step around him, but Bowie tightened his hold on her wrist and rose from the dressing bench to stand in front of her.

"You're incredible!" she muttered. "Totally incredible!"

"And if you quit, what is that going to make you? A nurse who was incapable of handling her patient?"

Incensed, she stared at him. "That's a low blow, Bowie. Really low."

Ashamed of himself, he eased his hold on her wrist and slowly slid his hand up her forearm. Even with an angry glare on her face, it was heavenly to touch her, to be close enough to smell her perfume, to feel the heat of her body.

"You're right. And I'm sorry. This time I do mean it. And I don't want you to leave. You're the first woman to—" Unsure of how to go on without making a gushing fool of himself, he turned away from her and swiped a hand over his face. To his surprise, he found his fingers were trembling.

What was happening to him? In spite of his injuries, he wasn't physically weak. Not to the point of having the shakes.

"The first woman to what?" she prompted.

"Nothing. I don't know why I said that." He twisted back to her. "Ava, there's something going on between us. You know it as well as I do."

His gaze picked up the flare of her nostrils, then dropped to her lips. The kiss had left them puffy, and the rose-colored lipstick she'd been wearing earlier was now gone. Bowie wished he had every right to lean into her and kiss her all over again.

"That's another reason why you need a different nurse," she said tersely. "I—I've hardly been behaving like a professional."

"That's my fault. Not yours," he said quickly.

"All the same, I—"

Wrapping his hands around her upper arms, he leaned toward her. "I'll behave myself, Ava. Just promise you won't quit. I need you."

Her expression turned cynical. "Anybody can change a bandage. That's all you need."

"If that's all there was to it, then I'd get my brother or dad to take care of me."

She leveled a stern look at him. "Those burns are serious, Bowie."

And so was the way she made him feel, Bowie thought. Yet he was smart enough to keep that bit of information to himself. She wasn't ready to hear it. She might never be ready. But he wanted the chance to know her better, to find out exactly what this electricity between them was all about.

"That's why I need you. To make sure they keep healing."

Groaning, she turned her head to one side and Bowie's gaze was drawn to her slender throat. He wanted to kiss her there. Just as much as he wanted to kiss her lips again.

"I don't know why I'm doing this," she said quietly. "And it's against my better judgment, but I'll give this one more try. But we are going to be patient and nurse. Nothing else. Understand?"

Relief poured through him, and Bowie wondered if he was going crazy. No woman should be having this much effect on him. Especially a widow who wanted nothing to do with him. Or did she? Her kiss had certainly said there was something she liked about him.

"What about friends?" he asked. "We can be that, can't we?"

She studied him for long moments and then finally a smile of surrender spread across her face. "Friends. Just friends."

"Great."

He maneuvered his way around the dressing bench and took a seat with his back to her.

"What are you doing now?" she wanted to know.

"I think the front of me is pretty clean. But you haven't done my back."

A stretch of silence passed before he felt the washcloth between his shoulder blades. As water rolled down his backbone, he grinned to himself.

Ava Archer was quite a woman.

Ava had just stepped out of the shower the next morning when she heard the phone ringing. Annoyed at the interruption, she hurriedly dried off, but before she could finish wrapping a fleece robe around her, the ringing stopped.

Out in the bedroom, she checked the call log on the nightstand phone and was surprised to see the caller had been her mother.

Since Velda Archer rarely called her daughter at this time of the morning, Ava decided she'd better check in.

Velda answered cheerfully on the second ring. "Good morning, honey. Did I wake you?"

"I was in the shower. Is anything wrong?"

"No. I just wanted to ask you about your plans for Christmas."

Ava sank onto the edge of the bed. "Christmas? Mother, it's only the fourth of December. The holiday is a long way off yet."

"Not as far as your father and I are concerned."

Even though Ava's parents had been divorced for the past ten years, they spent more time together than they did apart. They clearly loved each other, yet they couldn't live under the same roof for more than two weeks at a time.

"Oh, so what do you two have planned?"

"I'm leaving this morning for San Diego. Stu has a bunch of things planned for us to do. Including a trip up to Santa Anita."

"And probably a trip down Rodeo Drive. Like a shopping trip," Ava added sagely.

Velda laughed. "Honey, you know your father isn't that rich. Comfortable, but hardly rich enough to shop on Rodeo Drive. Still, he's promised he has a nice surprise hidden away for my Christmas gift. I'm guessing jewelry. He knows how much I love diamonds."

Even though her mother couldn't see her, Ava shook

her head in wry disbelief. "Along with emeralds, sap-
phires, rubies and any other colored stone known to man.
Mother, you're shameless. You won't sleep with Dad, yet
you'll accept his gifts."

There was a long pause before Velda laughed. "Not
sleep with him? Ava, where in the world did you get that
idea? Sex is the best thing we have going for us."

Leave it to her mother to be so blunt. "But you two
are divorced."

"What's that got to do with it? A piece of paper hasn't
altered our feelings for each other. It just means if we
try to live with each other twenty-four hours of every
day, then I start getting on his nerves and he starts getting on mine."

"That's not the way I'd want things. If I had a husband…" Ava's words trailed away as feelings of emptiness swept over her.

Velda groaned. "Oh, honey, Lawrence has been dead
for a long, long time. When are you going to start thinking about the future? About yourself and your needs?"

Emotion thickened her throat, forcing her to swallow.
"I am thinking about the future. And I have all I need. A
job I love. A house. Two loving parents and a few good
friends. What else could I possibly want?"

"What else? Really, Ava?"

Ava closed her eyes and remembered back to when
she'd still been a young wife and the future had spanned
before her like a bright ribbon of sunshine. Lawrence
had planned to stay in the military just long enough to
finish his college education. Once that was behind him,
he could get a normal day job, and they could put down
roots and start a family. But Lawrence had fallen in love
with the army and wanted to make it his career. She'd

argued and pleaded with him, to no avail. Lawrence had reenlisted and her dreams had ultimately died with him.

"Mother, you called me about Christmas. Not to hound me about my marital status."

"Right. God forgive a mother for mentioning such a taboo subject to her daughter."

Ava had always had a great relationship with both her parents. And most of the time, she didn't pay any attention to her mother's urgings for her to find a husband. But she wasn't in the mood this morning. Not when she had to face Bowie again. Just thinking about seeing him half-undressed with that love-me grin on his face was enough to make her want a stiff drink.

"I need to get dressed. I'm going to be late for work," she said. "I'll talk with you later about Christmas."

Ava walked over to an armoire and pulled a white uniform from its hanger.

"Well, it's no big deal. I mostly called to tell you I'll be spending the holiday with your father. We'd love for you to come down to San Diego and spend it with us. If you can't, that's okay, too. Have you already made plans?"

"Uh, no. I'll probably be working anyway."

"Ava! You—"

"Gotta go, Mother. Bye."

Ava ended the call and started across the room to gather her shoes from the closet, but something caused her to walk back to the nightstand. She opened the bottom drawer and pulled out a framed five-by-seven photo of Lawrence.

For years she'd kept the photo at her bedside, as a way to honor her late husband. The image was also a reminder that, at one point in her life, a man had loved and wanted her. But a few months ago, in a burst of self-determination, she'd finally made the decision to put the photo away. Now Ava wondered if she'd made a mistake. Last night she'd needed the comforting image of Lawrence's face. She'd lain awake for hours thinking about Bowie, dreaming about his kiss and how just the touch of his hand had turned her hot and weak with desire.

In the next hour and a half she was going to have to face the firefighter again. And though she'd insisted the two of them could only be friends, her thoughts of the man had nothing to do with friendship and everything to do with making love.

## Chapter Four

Bowie had been drinking his first cup of coffee when his grandfather Bart had walked through the bedroom door. Since then, the two men had been sitting in a pair of armchairs overlooking the busy ranch yard and talking about the family business. Bart had been subtly hinting at the prospect of Bowie becoming a part of ranch operations, but so far Bowie had managed to dodge any direct questions. Yet he realized that the closer he got to being completely healed, the more Bart would start pushing. Bowie had to be prepared to resist.

But for now, the two men hadn't reached such an impasse. Bowie was simply enjoying the private time with his grandfather. Bart had always seemed bigger than life to him, and to most of the people on the western slope of Nevada. Now, at the ripe age of eighty-five, he was still a stout mountain of a man, with thick gray hair and a granite jaw. Bowie hoped he would always have his grandfather's courage and strength.

"Granddad, when you met Grandmother, how did you know she was the right woman? The one you wanted to spend the rest of your life with?"

Now why had that question come out of his mouth, Bowie wondered. Was it because he'd spent half of last night thinking about Ava? Wondering what it was about her that turned him into a randy fool?

Bart let out a sly chuckle. "Now, what's a young stud like you asking an old man like me about women?"

Bowie felt a warm blush rush over his face. "Well, I guess talking with you about the ranch has brought back memories. You and Grandmother were together for so many years. And you seemed like you were in love with each other right up until she passed away. That doesn't happen with most couples nowadays. I just wondered how you pulled it off."

Clearly pleased by his grandson's observations, Bart smiled with fond remembrance. "I was crazy in love with that woman from the very first glance. And I can honestly say our love grew stronger with time."

"So it was love at first sight. That surprises me, Granddad. From everything I've seen, you've always been a man who carefully weighed your decisions. How did you first meet Grandmother?"

Bart's eyes twinkled as he rubbed his chin. "My dad—your great-grandfather Gorman—forced the whole family to attend a local social function. It was one of those things about cattlemen and politicians and raising money. Boring stuff to a young guy barely out of his teens. I wanted to go to a bar with my buddies, drink beer and pick up girls."

Bowie grinned at the image of Bart roaming the town. "You did that sort of thing back then?"

Bart chuckled. "Hell, Bowie. You think I was always like I am now? Back then I was like you—young and full of vinegar. But back to Gilda, your grandmother—she was at that boring party. Dancing with another guy. But I never paid any mind to him. The moment I laid eyes on her I knew I had to have her."

"So how hard was it for you to win her over?" Bowie asked.

"Damned hard. It took me a long time to convince her I was serious. But once I did, she gave me her heart."

Was that what Bowie wanted from Ava—her heart? When she'd walked into his bedroom that first morning, he'd felt punched in the gut, too. But that didn't mean he'd suddenly found the love of his life. It just meant he'd felt a wild, instant attraction. That's all it had been.

"You were lucky, Granddad," Bowie told him.

Bart rose from the chair and stretched. "No, Bowie, I was blessed. When you figure out the difference, you'll know when you've found the right woman."

Bowie was trying to digest his grandfather's sage advice when a knock sounded on the door and Ava stepped into the room.

Bowie pushed himself to his feet while Bart walked over to greet her.

"Hello, Ms. Archer," Bart said as he held a hand out to Ava. "Nice to see you again."

Smiling warmly, Ava shook his grandfather's hand. "It's very nice to see you, too, Mr. Calhoun. You look as though you're doing very well."

"Never better," he happily replied, then glanced over

to Bowie. "How's my grandson? Think he's going to survive?"

Ava looked over to Bowie and as their gazes met he felt a soft kick to his midsection.

"He'll have a few scars to wear, but he'll survive," she said.

"Well, the whole family certainly appreciates the care you're giving our boy," Bart told her. "And now, if you two will excuse me, I've got to go see a man about a horse."

The old expression had Bowie staring at his grandfather. "Granddad! You're not supposed to be drinking anymore!" Bowie scolded.

Laughing loudly, Bart started toward the door. "Bowie, it's time you remember you're living on a ranch. I'm not going after a bottle of bourbon. I'm actually talking about a horse! A stallion. Orin and I think we've found the right one. So we're going to go have a look at him."

Still chuckling, Bart left the bedroom and once he'd shut the door behind him, Bowie walked over to Ava. The white dress she was wearing this morning was different from the one she'd had on yesterday. It was straight and close fitting and covered with a lacy white sweater. Her dark hair was piled atop her head in a messy group of curls. The vibrant shade of her lips stood out against her ivory skin, like dark red cherries in a bowl of cream.

Bowie was convinced she was the sexiest woman he'd ever seen in his life. That's why he was feeling punched in the gut, he decided. It wasn't the same sort of thing that his grandfather had felt for his grandmother. No, that was something different. Something Bowie wasn't ready to feel.

"Good morning," he cheerfully greeted her. "Are the

roads better today? From what I can see out the window it looks like some of the snow melted off yesterday."

"They're much better." She stepped around him and carried her medical bag over to the nightstand. "I'm a bit late because I was detained with a phone call."

"Doesn't matter. There's no need for you to stick to a strict time schedule. I'm not like Granddad. I don't need to go see a man about a horse."

Smiling, she walked over to him. "It's nice to see a man your grandfather's age interested in his work and still able to do it."

"Granddad still rides. And I hope when it comes his time to go, that's where he'll be. In the saddle. Doing what he loves most."

Her expression turned soft and serious. "And what would you like to be doing when you leave this world? Fighting fires? If so, you almost got your wish a few weeks ago."

He grinned at her in an effort to lighten the moment. "But that didn't happen. I'm still here. And I have a treat for you. Have you eaten breakfast yet?"

Her eyes narrowed skeptically. "No. But I—"

"Great," he interrupted and with a hand on her arm, urged her over to the big armchair where his grandfather had been sitting. "Come over here and sit down. A few minutes ago Tessa brought up some of Greta's famous cinnamon rolls and a thermos of coffee."

"Is that why your grandfather was visiting? To have breakfast with you?"

Bowie chuckled. "Granddad gets up at five and has breakfast shortly after dawn. Besides, Greta would never let him have cinnamon rolls. She keeps a watch on his cholesterol. He had a stroke a few years back. Now he leaves the alcohol alone—or so he says—and tries to stick to his diet."

Ava sat down in the comfortable chair and smoothed the hem of her skirt. Bowie could've kept standing there staring at her legs, but he forced himself to turn his back and hobble over to the chair angled closely to her left.

On a table wedged between their chairs sat a thermos shaped like a large teapot. Next to it was another insulated container filled with warm cinnamon rolls. Bowie poured two cups of coffee and handed her one.

"There's cream and sugar if you like," he offered.

She fixed her coffee. "This is very nice, Bowie. But it's hardly your place to supply my breakfast. Besides, I don't normally eat much. A piece of toast at the most."

He handed her a plate with a cinnamon roll. "Shame on you. Being a nurse, you should know you need to start the day with more nutrition than that."

"True. But nurses and doctors don't always follow their own advice."

She took a forkful of the cinnamon roll and Bowie waited for her reaction before he dug into his own roll.

"Mmm. If everything else Greta cooks tastes this good, then I can see why she's been the family cook for so long."

"Greta thinks of herself as more than a cook for the Calhouns. She's more like a second grandmother to us brothers."

She cast him a thoughtful glance. "Lilly told me that Bart's wife died several years ago. What about your maternal grandparents? Are they still living?"

He nodded. "Alice and Tuck Reeves. They live over in the Virginia City area. Pops served as sheriff of Storey County for more than twenty years. Granny retired from school teaching. Now they stay busy doing charity work. And Pops keeps a few cattle and a couple of horses just for something to keep him busy."

"Hmm. So your grandfather Reeves was a sheriff. He obviously liked living dangerously, too."

Bowie shrugged. "I don't know that I'd call it dangerous. But he liked to kick ass. Uh, sorry. You know, collar the bad guys and make sure they remained behind bars."

"Yes, I do know," she said succinctly. "Lawrence was all about going after the bad guys."

"So your husband was the gung-ho sort?"

Nodding, she averted her gaze from him and sighed. Bowie couldn't tell whether her reaction was from sadness or frustration.

"That's right. Other than me and his mother, everyone called him Larry. And being a soldier was everything to him. Don't get me wrong. He didn't want to be a hero. But he wanted to be in the middle of the action. Always. That's what killed him." Shaking her head, she gave him a wan smile. "But I don't want to talk about any of that right now. I'd rather enjoy this delicious breakfast."

Bowie watched her sip the coffee and wondered what it would be like to have her always sitting across from him at the breakfast table. Even more, what would it be like to have her lying in his arms through the night? To wake up and find her next to him?

Endearing though they were, the images were disturbing to Bowie. Because they were thoughts of a man on a one-way track, with only one woman traveling with him.

"So are you getting excited about Christmas coming?" he asked, determined to divert his thoughts. "My family always makes a big deal of the holiday. What about yours?"

"My parents are going to be in San Diego for Christmas, so I won't be spending it with them. And my brother lives in Redding, California, so I'll probably just give him a call."

"What about grandparents? Are yours living?"

"They are, but both sets live out of state. I only see them during the summer. Usually my mother's parents come to Lake Tahoe and vacation. Dad's folks spend a few weeks up in Reno to gamble and see the sights."

"So you won't be spending your Christmas with family," he mused aloud. "That sounds lonely. Unless you have big plans with friends."

"No plans. I usually offer to work. That gives some of the nurses with children a chance to have time off."

She had no husband or children to share the festivities. Neither did he. But the comparison wasn't the same. Rafe had been right when he'd said Ava was a family-type woman. When Bowie looked at her he saw her as a wife and mother, too. That ought to be more than enough to squash his dreams of kissing her again. Unfortunately, it wasn't.

"That's admirable," Bowie told her. "But I hope you'll decide to do some celebrating this year. It's my first Christmas back on the Silver Horn. I'd like for you to spend some of it with me—uh, us Calhouns."

She looked taken aback, as though he'd lost his mind. Or that he'd stepped over that invisible line of hers again.

"That's not going to happen," she said firmly.

"Why?"

She placed her empty plate on the little table, then clutched the coffee cup with both hands. "First of all, I'm hired help. You shouldn't be bringing me into family situations, celebrations or anything else."

"Really? Then why did you attend the christening parties for Lilly and Rafe's children? Those were definitely family affairs."

A soft pink color stained her cheeks and Bowie tried to remember the last woman he'd seen blush. Frankly, he couldn't recall one. Did that mean he'd been going out with overly confident women? Or was Ava simply that different from the generation he normally dated?

"I wasn't working for your family then," Ava pointed out. "And Lilly is my friend."

He grinned at her. "What about me? I thought we were going to be friends."

He watched her gaze scan his face, then settle on his lips. No doubt she was thinking about that kiss they'd shared yesterday. Was she regretting it? Or was she, like him, longing to repeat it?

She said, "Well, I suppose we are...friends. But I'm still your nurse." She placed the cup alongside her empty plate and rose to her feet. "And we should start on changing your bandages. I need to be getting back to Carson City soon."

So she wanted to get this visit over with. Bowie shouldn't feel disappointed. Especially since she'd taken the time to sit down and have coffee with him. Yet those few minutes weren't enough for him. He wanted to spend hours with her. A night with her. But he wasn't going to press her for anything right now. Slow and easy. He figured that was the only way he could ever catch Ava.

"Okay. I'll let you get to work."

He pushed himself out of the chair and reached for his crutch.

She cast him a skeptical look. "What's this? No delay tactics?"

"No. I'm sure you have plenty to do once you get back to town. And like you said, you aren't here for my entertainment."

He sat down on the edge of the bed and began to unbutton his shirt.

With a skeptical look, she watched while he shrugged out of the denim shirt. "Is this some sort of trick?"

"I'm not a fun-and-games person all the time, Ava. I can be serious."

Her expression still doubtful, she walked over to him. "And was it the fun-and-games side of you that kissed me yesterday?"

"Is that what it felt like to you?" he asked softly.

She took a step back, as though she feared he was going to reach for her again. Or could it be that she wanted to reach for him? Was he crazy to think the smoky look in her eyes was desire?

She said, "I asked first."

He must have been out of his mind to think he could take things slowly with this woman. She wasn't some ingenue. In fact, she got straight to the point long before he did.

"Okay. It was the serious side of me," he admitted.

She said nothing to that. Instead, she scanned his face for a moment longer, then quietly went to work on his shoulder.

"Are you angry at me again?" he asked.

"No. I'm just trying to decide whether to believe you."

"Well, you can believe this, Ava. Right now I'd like to pull you down on this bed with me and make love to you."

He felt her fingers pause against his shoulder before she muttered, "I'm going to pretend I didn't hear that."

"Pretend all you want," he told her. "I figure you've been doing that for a long time now, anyway."

When Ava finally left Bowie's bedroom and started down the long staircase, she was still thinking about his remarks.

So he thought she was going through life pretending. The thought had her inwardly seething. What did he know about her life? A week ago he'd never met her. No doubt he'd only made that remark to prod her into some sort of defensive reaction. But she'd not given him the satisfaction. Instead she'd checked his leg and foot for swelling, medicated his burns, applied new bandages and even sponge bathed him before helping him back into his shirt.

It didn't matter that touching him had sent her heart pounding and heat pulsing through every cell of her body. She needed to hide her response to him. She had to make him see there was no chance on this earth that she would ever fall into bed with him.

"Ava! Oh, I'm so glad I caught you."

The sound of Lilly's voice broke into her thoughts. Glancing down, she spotted her friend standing at the bottom of the staircase, her hand resting on the ornately carved balustrade.

"Lilly. How nice to see you." She hurried down the steps to give her friend a warm hug. "I've been wondering if I might run into you."

The pretty blonde gave Ava a bright smile. "I've been working the clinic for the past few days. I normally work Wednesday through Friday, but one of the other nurses needed time off, so we switched."

Ava glanced eagerly around her. "So where are the kiddies?"

"In the family room sitting under the Christmas tree. Colleen is trying to explain to her little brother about Santa. He just doesn't get it yet. Except the word *toys*," Lilly added with a laugh. "Do you have time to go see them?"

"I'll make time."

The two women started down a hallway. As they walked, Lilly asked, "How's the ER going?"

"Busy as ever. Do you ever miss it?"

Lilly shrugged. "I'll be honest, sometimes I do. But the grind would kill me now. I couldn't work the ER and give my babies or husband the attention they deserve. And they're my first priority."

Yes, Lilly had a handsome husband who adored her and two beautiful children. She had a full life outside nursing now. Ava couldn't imagine how that would feel.

"Well, I miss working with you. But I'm glad you're so happy. By the way, do you see Marcella much nowadays?"

Marcella was another nurse who had worked the ER with Ava and Lilly. But a couple of years ago, her growing family had forced her to move to a different job.

"I try to see her fairly often. She's working full-time at the women's health center. You know, being a single mother with two growing boys, things are financially tight for her. She works a lot of overtime, but sometimes a person has to make sacrifices."

"I remember when she adopted little Peter," Ava said thoughtfully. "I worried then that she was taking on too much."

A wan smile touched Lilly's face. "Yes. But she loves him so. And that's all that really matters to her."

Yes, Ava supposed, love was the thing that mattered most. But she didn't have a husband or children to love. Her house was empty. There was no man yelling for a clean pair of socks, or siblings fighting over the last bowl of cereal. There were no babies to feed and rock. No husband to hold her after the children were asleep and the house was dark and quiet.

The two women took a right and after a few steps down another hallway entered an arched entryway into the family room.

The instant Colleen spotted her mother, she jumped up and raced toward them. "Mommy! Mommy! Autin crying!"

The girl grabbed her mother's hand and began tugging her over toward a huge decorated fir tree where her little brother was playing on the floor with a set of plastic animals, along with a miniature truck and horse van.

"Austin is crying? Your little brother looks okay to me," Lilly assured her daughter.

Across the room, Tessa looked up from dusting an upright piano. "Austin was yelling a moment ago. Because his sister told him that Santa couldn't put horses under the tree. Apparently that's what your son wants for Christmas."

Laughing, Lilly bent down to her daughter's level and patiently explained, "Colleen, your brother is too small to get a pony. Santa knows the right gift to bring Austin."

"I wouldn't be so sure," Tessa spoke up. "Uh, I overhead Rafe and Bart discussing a pony. I'm pretty sure they were going to talk to Santa about one."

Rising to her full height, Lilly urged her daughter to

go play with her brother before she glanced over at the maid. "Oh, please, Tessa, tell me you're kidding."

Tessa shook her head, and Ava smiled at Lilly's look of dismay.

"I wouldn't worry," Ava told her. "At least Santa can't leave a pony under the tree. He'll have to make a visit to the barn."

"That's a comforting thought," Lilly said with a good-natured laugh, then gestured over to a long plush couch facing the Christmas tree. "Let's sit. I'm really glad I caught you this morning, Ava. I wanted to talk to you about Bowie."

Ava mentally stiffened as she took a seat. After the tense minutes she'd just spent with Bowie, she needed to get the man off her mind, not discuss him. But Bowie was a part of Lilly's family. It was only natural for her to be interested in the progress of his condition.

"Actually, his burns are coming along nicely. No infection. No fever. It's just going to take time for his skin to rejuvenate. As for his ankle, the best I can tell, there's not much swelling in his leg or toes, so that's encouraging."

Lilly sighed. "That's all well and good. It's the healing time that has me worried. If Bowie can't start getting out and about, he's either going to turn into a monster or slip into a depression. Did he mention to you that he went out with Rafe a couple of days ago? They drove out to one of the west ranges on the ranch to where the fence crew was working. Rafe promised he'd make Bowie stay in the truck, but once those two get out of sight, who knows what they do. They both think they're invincible."

Ava's expression turned serious. "Lilly, I don't have to tell you what would happen if Bowie got bacteria in those wounds. Even if he stayed in the truck, the dirt and manure and—"

"Believe me, Ava, I tried to stop them," Lilly interrupted. "But Rafe wouldn't hear of it. He's worried about Bowie's spirits, and frankly, I am, too."

"Being confined comes with injuries. And being mentally strong enough to deal with that is a major part of the healing process."

"True. That's why I want to keep Bowie's spirits high. What do you think about him going to town to the Grubstake and having coffee with old friends?"

"He isn't allowed to drive."

"That's not an issue. One of his brothers or a ranch hand could drive him," Lilly suggested.

Ava shrugged and hoped she looked like a professional RN instead of a woman worrying about her man. Because Bowie wasn't her man. Still, she wanted him to be more than healthy. She also wanted him to be happy.

"I see what you're getting at, Lilly. But being out in a public place right now would be asking for trouble. Especially at this time of year, when flu germs are making the rounds."

Lilly nodded glumly. "That concern had crossed my mind, too. I guess I just wanted to hear you say I was being overly cautious. But he could, at least, come downstairs and have supper with his family."

Lilly's comment caused Ava to arch her brows. "As long as he gets help maneuvering the stairs. He hasn't been leaving his room?"

"Not yesterday." She frowned thoughtfully. "Rafe and I think he's using his condition to keep his distance and avoid the family routine."

Ava shook her head. "I don't understand. I got the impression Bowie loves his family."

Lilly grimaced. "Oh, he does. But the more we try to draw him into the family circle, the more he starts to squirm."

"I understand he's been living here since he returned from military duty. He ought to be comfortable around all of you," Ava reasoned.

"That's true in a sense. But with training for the hotshot crew and fighting fires, he's mostly gone from the ranch. Sticking around all the time and being a part of family life isn't his style. Rafe and I are afraid he's going to start ignoring doctor's orders and do things that might jeopardize his recovery."

Just hearing Lilly talk about Bowie's desire for a life on the go made Ava even more determined to keep their relationship from developing into anything more than friendship. If—and it was a mighty big *if*—she ever decided she was ready to fall in love again, she was going to make sure it wasn't with a young, untamed man like Bowie.

"You need to relax, Lilly. Bowie is a strong-minded guy. He's not going to let any of this get him down." She rose to her feet and gave her friend a warm smile. "I'd like to stay longer, but I need to get home. I have a ton of things to do before work this evening."

Lilly stood. "I could talk for hours, but I've not forgotten what it's like to work six or seven days a week. So I won't try and keep you." She looked over at the maid. "Tessa, would you watch the kids a minute while I walk Ava to the door?"

"Oh, there's no need for that," Ava quickly insisted, then leaned over and gave her friend a kiss on the cheek.

"I'll see my way out. And before my assignment with Bowie is over with, I'm sure we'll have a chance to visit many times."

Lilly smiled impishly. "Yes. We'll make a point to."

During Ava's visits over the next three days, Bowie was mostly quiet and pensive. And, as crazy as it seemed, she had to admit she missed the Bowie she'd first met. The one who'd flirted shamelessly. The one with a gleam in his eye and a sexy grin on his face.

His behavior in those first few meetings had made her feel like a woman again, had reminded her of all she'd been missing since Lawrence had died. And because she'd been too much of a coward to handle those feelings, she'd drawn a line between the two of them. Since then Bowie had remained on his side of the dividing line. She should be pleased about that. Instead, she was miserable.

These past three days Ava had thought of little more than Bowie. When she woke in the mornings, he was on her mind, and each night, before sleep finally overtook her weary brain, he was the last image she envisioned. Today, on her drive to the Silver Horn, she'd finally reached the conclusion that it was time she stopped running from the feelings he evoked in her and face them head-on.

"I got a surprise today," she said to Bowie as she carefully applied medication to the burn on his rib cage. "A fellow nurse wanted to pull my shift tonight so that later this month I could fill in for her. That means I have the night off."

"It also means the closer you get to Christmas, the more you'll have to work."

Ava had never heard him speak in such a sardonic

way, and she wondered if Lilly might be right. Perhaps the seclusion of the ranch was getting under his skin. Or perhaps he was simply becoming bored with her visits. One thing was for sure. Ever since he'd talked about pulling her down on the bed and making love to her, everything between them had changed.

"Probably," she said. "But that's okay. I don't mind."

"Little Miss Perfect," he said, his voice slathered with sarcasm. "Must be great to always do right and good."

Stepping back, she stabbed him with a nasty glare. "So I'm finally seeing the real Bowie Calhoun. The one who whines about his lot in life and beats up everybody else so they'll be just as wretched as he is."

He heaved out a heavy breath and raked a hand over his tawny-gold hair. "I'm not whining," he protested. "But I'm sorry. You didn't deserve that."

She folded her arms against her breasts as she carefully studied his face. He looked bored and tired and miserable and Ava hated seeing him this way. "You know, just before you came out with that sweet observation, I was about to ask if you felt like going out tonight. But you don't much look like you're up to it. Going out, that is."

Curiosity arched one brow. "Out? Where?"

"Don't get too excited. I'm not talking about a nightclub or anything you'd consider fun."

"Then what?"

Ava's gaze met his. "Dinner at my house."

From the look on his face, she'd clearly stunned him. "Who else is going to be there?"

"No one. Just the two of us."

His brows pulled together in a frown of disbelief. "What is this about?"

"It's about thinking you might enjoy getting away from this room and the ranch for a while."

He grimaced. "You aren't responsible for my entertainment, remember? So why are you doing this?"

Because she wanted to know why he was consuming her every thought. Was it simply carnal lust she felt for the man? Or something more? How would she ever know if she didn't spend time with him? But she wasn't about to let him in on her real motives. He'd either be amused or inclined to take advantage.

"Two reasons. First of all, I enjoy cooking. And secondly, I don't like eating alone."

His eyes narrowed skeptically. "And I'm supposed to believe there's not another man around who wouldn't jump at the chance to be your dinner partner? Come on, Ava. I'm not stupid."

"No, you're not stupid. But you're definitely rude, asking all these questions. Either accept the invitation or thank me and decline. It's entirely up to you."

The look on his face said he wasn't used to a woman giving him any sort of ultimatum. Ava figured when it came to the opposite sex, he expected to always have the upper hand. He had a lot to learn.

She turned away from him long enough to fetch clean bandage material from the nightstand. By the time she turned back, a wide grin marked his face and the sight sent joy rippling through Ava.

He said, "No matter your reasons, Ava, I'd be honored to have dinner with you."

"I'm glad," she murmured, then breaking eye contact, she went to work. "I'll try not to burn anything."

He chuckled and Ava thought how good it was to hear him laugh again, to see a smile on his face. Maybe she was acting like a foolish girl rather than a thirty-five-year-old widow, but for once she didn't care.

"Burn? I hope to heck we don't have to talk about burns tonight," he joked.

She lifted her head to look at him and as their gazes connected, her heart jumped into a wild gallop. "I'm sure we can find something else to talk about."

His gaze settled on her lips. "Or we don't have to talk at all," he suggested. "We could just…eat."

Ava had to force herself to breathe. "I was wondering how long it was going to take you to get back to your normal self."

Slowly his gaze eased upward until he was looking directly into her eyes, and the serious light Ava spotted in the green depths jolted her.

"I've just been waiting on you to decide which Bowie you liked the best. I'm glad you chose the real one, Ava."

He was right. She did like the real Bowie best. And that was a very scary thought.

## Chapter Five

When a Silver Horn ranch hand dropped Bowie off at Ava's house, darkness had settled over the quiet residential area. A street lamp shed enough light for him to make his way up a small stone walkway. Above the door, a dim light illuminated a tiny front porch made of concrete.

While he waited for Ava to answer his knock, he surveyed his surroundings. The wood-sided structure was small and L-shaped. The lap siding was painted white with gables and window shutters done in dark hunter green. A short driveway led up to the house, but there was no garage or carport. And as for the yard, there wasn't much to it, except for one Joshua tree growing near the walkway and some sort of shrub that sheltered part of the porch. The place was nice and neat, but something about it seemed lonely.

The sound of the opening door caught Bowie's attention and he turned to see Ava standing across the threshold. He could only stare at her, she was so beautiful in the dim light. Dressed in tight jeans and a thin black sweater, she wore her dark hair loose and it fell nearly to the middle of her back. She was smiling and the gleam of her white teeth against those cherry-red lips stirred a longing deep in his gut.

"Please come in," she invited warmly. "You timed it just right. I just took dinner out of the oven."

He held out a small ceramic pot planted with a Christmas cactus. "For you."

She appeared surprised that he'd bothered to bring a dinner gift, which made him wonder if the men she knew didn't bring her tokens of appreciation.

*Bowie, she doesn't do this with other men. Or so she says. She's a widow. Her dinner companion is just a memory. A ghost that she doesn't want to push out of her life.*

Her expression softened as she took the plant from him. "How beautiful. Thank you, Bowie."

"It's already making buds," Bowie said, his voice unusually husky. "Hopefully it will bloom by Christmas."

"Whether it blooms or not, I'll enjoy it," she assured him, then stepped to one side of the door and gestured for him to enter.

With the help of his crutch, he stepped past her and into the house. The small living room felt blessedly warm, and the delicious aroma of dinner drifted to his nostrils. While she dealt with the door, his glance took in a green leather couch, a matching armchair and the pinewood floor.

"I thought I was going to be late," he said. "Frank, the ranch hand who drove me into town, thinks he's speeding if he goes more than fifty-five miles an hour."

She placed the cactus on a low glass-topped coffee table before gesturing to his jacket and cowboy hat. "If you'd like I'll put those away for you."

It had been a long time since he'd dressed like a cowboy. The close-fitting jeans and Western shirt felt totally different than the loose fatigues he'd worn so many years in the Marines. And he'd had to split the seam at the bottom of his jean leg in order to pull it over the bulky cast. But the appreciative glance Ava had given him made him glad he'd made the effort to look decent tonight.

"If I can get balanced," he told her, "I'll try to get out of this jacket."

"You can't do that with a crutch under your arm." She leaned the metal support against the back of an armchair before she reached for the zipper on his jacket. "If you start to lose your balance, just grab my arm."

As she moved around him, her flowery perfume mixed with the aroma of the food. It was a comforting scent that took him back to Sunday dinners at home, with his mother still wearing her church clothes and Bowie and his brothers waiting to pounce on a platter of fried chicken. At that time he'd not recognized how special those days were, but he certainly did now.

Ava carried his things over to a small closet. "Are you ready to eat? Or if you'd like, we can have a drink first. I have a bottle of wine, ginger ale, soda or fruit juice. Just take your pick."

"Thanks, but I really don't need a drink. Unless you do."

"I'm fine. So we'll get started with our meal, then." She handed him the crutch and motioned for him to follow. "Sorry, my little house doesn't have a separate dining room. Everything is in the kitchen."

As Bowie watched her go, he wondered how he was going to keep his senses straight and his hands to himself. "I'm used to eating most anywhere," he assured her. "Sitting on the floor or the ground. Outside. Inside. Wherever."

They passed through a short hallway before turning left into a cozy kitchen equipped with stainless steel appliances and a white farm table.

Ava pulled out a chair at one end and Bowie wished like hell he wasn't dragging around a crutch. His father and grandfathers had ingrained manners into him and his brothers, and right now he wanted to be the one helping her into her chair.

"Have a seat," she told him, "and I'll finish putting the rest of our meal on the table. What would you like to drink? We're having lasagna, so you might like the wine with it."

"No, thanks. Water will be good."

She placed a large baking dish on the table and the smell of melted cheese and marinara sauce nearly had his mouth watering.

"Do you have something against alcohol?" she asked curiously. "Or you just don't like it?"

"I drink a beer now and then, but not much more. Some of my military buddies drank too much. I guess watching them make fools of themselves put me off. And then Grandfather Bart has had his problems with the stuff, too." He looked at her. "What about your late husband? Did he drink?"

Her lips tight, she placed glasses of ice water next to their plates. "A bit too much. Because of me, I'm afraid."

"Why? He worried about leaving you alone?"

"No. I was constantly hounding him to get out of the army. And he didn't want to get out."

Bitterness tinged her voice and Bowie wondered if it was directed at herself or her late husband. Either way, he wasn't about to press her about the subject and ruin this special evening.

"Sorry. I wasn't trying to pry. Really."

"Forget it. Let's eat," she urged him. "Would you like salad?"

"Sure."

She filled a bowl with fresh greens and cherry tomatoes and passed it to him. Bowie poured a healthy amount of dressing over the vegetables and sprinkled it all with black pepper.

"So how does it feel to be off the ranch?" she asked.

"Nice. Real nice."

She offered him a basket filled with slices of toasted Italian bread. "I'm glad you came."

The faint smile on her face was as enticing as a full moon hanging over the edge of a mountaintop, making it impossible to concentrate on the food in front of him.

"I'm glad I did, too," he told her.

This was the first time he'd seen her in something other than a nurse's uniform, and the casual clothing made her look entirely different. Dressed as a nurse, she was beautiful and feminine, but like this, she was a sexy vixen.

"So have you lived in this house for very long?" he asked.

"About ten years." She cast him a wan smile. "Compared to your home it's like a matchbox. But it's plenty of space for me. And best of all, it's mine."

He shook his head. "You probably think I'm accustomed

to living in luxury, but I'm not. These past years I've lived in barracks and military housing. As far as I'm concerned your house is nice and comfortable."

"And you're being kind." She ate a few bites of salad before she said, "I can honestly say that before I took on the job of nursing you, I'd never been in a house as huge or elaborate as your family home."

"It wasn't always that big. When my great-grandfather first started the ranch in 1901, he built a four-room log cabin. He started adding on to it when he and my great-grandmother started having children."

Interest lit her features. "So your grandfather Bart had siblings?"

"Two sisters and a brother. His sisters married young and moved away. Both of them died in recent years. His brother died from pneumonia when he was only a child." He took a drink of his water. "My father has a sister, Arlene. She lives in Reno. His brother, Dave, was killed in the Vietnam War."

An empty look suddenly swept her face. "Ah, yes, war. Over the years it touches most families."

And it had touched hers in an overwhelming way, Bowie thought. Each time she mentioned her late husband, there was a lost expression in her eyes, a hint of pain in her voice. The reaction troubled Bowie greatly. She was too young and vibrant to be trapped in a tragic past and dwelling on memories.

He said, "The whole family is very proud of Uncle Dave's service to our country. You should be proud of Lawrence's, too. But I get the impression you aren't. I think you're embittered."

Her fork paused in midair as she shot him a look of resentment. "Since when did you become a psychiatrist?"

"You don't have to have a medical degree to have an opinion, Ava," he said wryly.

Her jaw clamped tight and Bowie braced himself for a lashing. But after a moment, her features relaxed and she turned her attention back to the food.

"There's so much history to your family and the ranch," she said. "It's hard for me to imagine being a part of something so big and long-lasting."

She was obviously changing the subject, but that was fine with Bowie. He was a guest in her home. He shouldn't be saying things to raise her hackles. Even if he was right.

"I'm lucky to have such a home and family. I'd be a fool not to recognize that," Bowie admitted. "But sometimes being a Calhoun can be a bit overwhelming."

Lifting her head, she studied his face. "Is that why you've chosen jobs that keep you away from the ranch and the family?"

To Bowie's dismay, her questions brought a guilty flush to his face. He told himself there was no reason to feel guilty. These past few years, he'd simply followed the path he'd chosen, not the one his family wanted for him.

He jabbed a fork into a tomato. "No. I chose to be a marine because I thought the job would fit me and give purpose to my life. It did. Now I'm a firefighter and so far it suits me. Not because it keeps me away from the ranch or my family, but because it challenges me."

"I'd bet the fact that it's dangerous and exciting had something to do with you choosing the hotshot crew," she said drily.

He grinned. "Why not? Life isn't meant to be boring. That's the way I see it."

"So once you're healed and back on your feet you plan to return to the hotshot crew?"

Her question jarred him. He'd figured that was already obvious to her and his whole family. On the other hand, he liked the fact that she was interested enough to ask. "Of course. Why wouldn't I?"

She shrugged and Bowie watched the shiny dark hair slide against her breasts and the image caused his brain to leap forward to a vision of Ava without her clothes and all that dark hair tumbling against her pale skin. The picture was more than enough to arouse him.

She began to speak and the sound of her voice jerked him out of the erotic fantasy. "When Orin first talked with me about being your nurse, he didn't say much about how or why you'd been hurt. But he did say that you were very close to being burned alive. He said if it hadn't been for the grace of God and your fellow firefighters, you wouldn't be here now. I would think that should be enough to give you second thoughts about returning. It would me."

"That's because you're a woman. You see danger differently than a man."

"Being a woman has nothing to do with it. I see danger for what it is. The risk of being hurt or killed."

So that was the issue with her, Bowie decided. Her husband had lost his life to a high-risk job. Now she couldn't see past that tragedy. A part of him could understand Ava's reasoning. Each time he climbed up or down the stairs at the ranch house, he remembered his mother. And he could only think that if he'd been at her side to hold her arm, to help and protect her, she wouldn't have fallen. Claudia Calhoun would be with her family today.

"Well, I don't believe my family fears for my life,

Ava. At least, none of them have ever expressed such concerns to me. What my family wants is for me to become a part of the ranch again—to be a cowboy alongside Rafe and Dad."

"What about Clancy? I understand he's the general manager of the Silver Horn. Does he ever do any cowboy work on the ranch? I mean, like roping and riding and that sort of thing."

"Clancy loves to get outdoors and join in on the physical work. Especially when it comes to spring roundup. But his job mainly keeps him shackled to the office."

"I see. And your other brother, Evan? Since he chose to be a deputy sheriff, I assume he doesn't like ranch work."

"Actually, Evan and his wife own a little ranch of their own. So when he isn't on duty as a deputy, he's doing cowboy work."

He pushed his salad aside and ladled a healthy portion of lasagna onto his plate. Across the table, he could see Ava's blue eyes studying him in a way that was unlike any woman he'd been with before. The fact that he'd noticed such a thing made Bowie a little uneasy. He didn't have serious conversations with women. He didn't bother to read their expressions or wonder what was going on behind their pretty faces. Until he'd met Ava, he'd simply enjoyed their beauty.

"Hmm. So that means all your brothers like cowboy work. Did you do much ranch work before you entered the Marines?"

"All of us brothers grew up learning how to rope and ride, fix fences, care for cattle and horses, and all the other things that go with ranching. Becoming a cowboy was required education in the Calhoun family."

"So you got the education. But you left the ranch before you put it to good use."

He shrugged, hoping she couldn't see that her comment had struck a nerve. He'd always been an easygoing guy and he'd never let himself think too deeply about things. But talking about leaving the ranch to enter the Marines bothered Bowie more than he cared to admit. A part of him had felt guilty to think of Clancy and Rafe and Finn working so hard to keep the family legacy going. True, Finn had gone his own way now, and Evan had chosen to be a detective with the sheriff's department rather than work on the Silver Horn, but that didn't justify Bowie's choices. That's why he'd not accepted any of the ranch's profits over the past nine years. The only dividends he'd agreed to receive were those that came from mining shares and other lucrative holdings in gas and oil.

"My brothers were naturals at ranching life. Especially Clancy, Rafe and Finn. I had to work extra hard at handling horses and cattle."

"And you didn't like being second best?" she prodded, then softened the question with a smile.

He caught himself proudly straightening his shoulders. "I don't like being second in anything. But that's not the reason I didn't hang around the Silver Horn. I just didn't believe I would be that much of an asset to the ranch."

A gentle smile tilted her lips. "Bowie, I believe you'd be an asset in whatever you chose to do."

The compliment surprised him. Especially since she seemed intent on labeling him a fun-loving daredevil.

"Thanks. But that's enough talk about me. Tell me about your nursing. How did you choose your career? Does anyone else in your family work in the medical field?"

She shook her head. "No. My mom just retired from a government secretarial job. She worked in the mayor's office here in Carson City for thirty years. Dad works for an investment firm down in San Diego. And as far as I know, there are no nurses or doctors on either side of the family. It was just something that called to me about the time I entered high school. So once I graduated, I went straight into nursing school. Lawrence and I got married when I was only twenty. After that I completed my studies to become an RN. I've been a nurse for thirteen years now."

"And you like it," he added.

She smiled. "Yes. It gets stressful at times, especially in the ER, but I like it."

"And what about outside jobs like me?" he asked. "Do you take on many of them?"

"In thirteen years, you're only the third patient I've cared for in their home. One was an elderly teacher recovering from a stroke. The other a child who'd contracted rubeola."

"Oh. I took it for granted that treating patients outside the hospital was something you did quite often."

"No. The home health care business has eased the need for home nurses."

"Twenty-four-hour RN care." He slanted a mischievous grin at her. "Don't you think I need that sort of care?"

Her cheeks turned a becoming pink. She pushed aside her salad bowl. "I think you're already getting all the care you need," she said primly.

Bowie chuckled. "Well, it never hurts for a man to try."

A faint smile tugged at the corners of her lips. "You are such a flirt."

"But you like it. Come on, admit it."

She glanced at him and Bowie spotted something in

her eyes that looked like desire. The notion thrilled him. And suddenly he felt like a very young man who'd never been touched by a woman. With Ava everything would be new and different and special.

"I like too much about you, Bowie."

"I like you, too, Ava. Very much."

By the time their meal was over and Ava had served Bowie coffee in the living room, she'd come to the conclusion that she'd made a giant mistake in inviting him to her home tonight. His presence was filling up each room, shoving away the lonely shadows and making her forget she was a widow.

*So what's wrong with forgetting, Ava? Isn't that what you've wanted to do for a long time now? Deep down haven't you wanted a man to come along and remind you that you were meant to be loved?*

*Loved.* That was the key word, Ava thought as she fought with the annoying voice in her head. Yes, she wanted to be loved again. That's why her attraction to Bowie was all wrong. Clearly he'd never loved a woman before, and it would be stupid of her to think he'd start with her.

"Are you planning on putting up a Christmas tree?" Bowie asked, interrupting her thoughts.

Careful to keep a cushion's distance between them, Ava joined him on the long couch. "Since it's just me and my time is limited, I doubt I'll put up a tree."

He looked disappointed. "That's a shame. You don't do a tree. You don't do parties. You don't even plan on being with your family. Doesn't Christmas mean anything to you?"

Ava frowned. "Of course it does. But it's not like I

have a big family with little kids running around getting ready for Santa to arrive. It's different for me."

He placed his cup on the coffee table and reached for his crutch. Ava said nothing as she watched him rise to his feet and walk over to a wall table holding several photos.

"Is this your family?"

He picked up one of the framed photos and Ava went to stand at his side. "That's my parents. Velda and Stuart. Most of their friends call them Vel and Stu."

"Did I hear you say they live in San Diego?"

"My father does. My mother lives here in Carson City. They're divorced. But they still spend a lot of time together."

"Hmm. So they're one of those couples that actually had an amicable divorce," he said.

"I think it's ridiculous," Ava admitted. "They love each other, but if they live together for more than a month at a time they start to bicker. I wish the two of them would realize how fortunate they are to have each other and quit focusing on silly things like leaving socks on the floor or not rinsing a coffee cup."

He placed the picture back on the table. "Yes, I think my father would tell them that very thing. Each moment is too precious to be wasted."

She'd not expected that sort of comment from Bowie, but she had to remember that as a teenager he'd lost his mother. She pointed to a photo next to her parents'.

"This is my brother, Tray. He's two years younger than me and works as a forest ranger in California."

"Is he married?"

"Was. He's divorced now. I guess it runs in the family."

"Not with you," he said gently.

"Lawrence and I were only married two years," she said quietly. "Not long enough for a divorce. But if he'd lived—well, I'd like to think it would have lasted. I guess I'm an old-fashioned girl."

He pointed to a five-by-seven photo framed in dark oak. "Is this your late husband?"

Dressed in combat fatigues, Lawrence was smiling and waving at the camera. The memory of that day was burned in Ava's brain.

"Yes. That was the day he was shipping out to Iraq. He was thrilled at the idea of seeing action. I was—well, I never saw him alive again. That was thirteen years ago."

"That's a long time," he said softly. "Too long for you to still be grieving."

She looked up at him. "How could you know what's the right or wrong length of time to grieve over a spouse? You've never had a wife."

His hand closed around her upper arm and the shock of his touch sent her heart into a breathless race.

"Ava, you just talked about your parents wasting time and how senseless it is. But look at yourself. Don't you want more?"

Her throat tight, she whispered, "I'll tell you the same thing I tell my mother. I have everything I want—for now."

His gaze slipped ever so slowly over her face until Ava felt herself trembling inside and out.

"Everything? You don't have this, do you?"

His husky voice shivered through her like the sound of rustling sheets, soft sighs and whispered promises.

"This?"

His gaze zeroed in on her lips and anticipation buzzed along her veins. "Yeah. This."

Ava wasn't sure if he was the one who reached for her or she for him. But once their lips met, it didn't matter which one of them had initiated the contact. The only important thing was that she was in his arms and he was kissing her again. And his lips were speaking a language she'd never heard before.

Hot and cold. Both sensations rushed through her at the same time, making sweat pop out on her upper lip and goose bumps rise up on her forearms. He tasted like a dark night full of danger and excitement and she was stunned at how much she wanted to keep on tasting him, how much she wanted to feel his hard, warm body press tighter and tighter against hers.

Across the room, she could hear the clock on the wall clicking away each second, while inside her head blood rushed loudly in her ears and a voice fought to rise above the heated turmoil.

*This man wants sex, Ava. Nothing more.*

So what was wrong with that? Ava kept up the mental argument. Wasn't a woman supposed to need physical satisfaction, too? She'd gone for years without a man to turn her body into a vessel of pleasure. How much longer should she go empty to make things right with her heart?

The tormenting questions were still roiling in her head when his mouth finally tore away from hers and his ragged breath brushed against her ear.

"Ava." He breathed her name as though he'd just unearthed a hidden treasure. "Kissing you is like—I don't know—it's like nothing I've ever felt before."

Tilting her head back, she gazed up at his face and her breath caught at the sober expression shadowing his eyes. She wasn't expecting that from him. No more than she was expecting to find herself shaking and wanting to grab hold of him and hang on tight.

"I hope you mean that in a good way," she said softly.

His hands slipped to the middle of her back and tugged her closer against him. "*Good* is not the word for it, Ava. It's incredible. Holding you, touching you like this—it's not like anything I expected. It's special. So special that I feel like something inside me is tearing apart."

He was describing the same shattering sensations going on inside her, and that frightened her right down to the core of her being.

She touched the lean angle of his cheekbone. "Oh, Bowie. This isn't supposed to be happening. I don't even know why I'm standing here this close to you. Or why I kissed you like—"

"Like you really wanted to kiss me," he finished for her.

Guilt, regret and loss were all suddenly tearing through her, jumbling her feelings into a mass of confusion.

"Yes. I wanted to kiss you. But you've already figured that out for yourself." With a heavy sigh, she pulled away from him and walked to the other side of the small room.

She was standing at the end of the couch, staring blindly at the wall, when he walked up behind her and rested his hands on her shoulders. The heat from his fingers radiated through her and she could only imagine how heady it would feel to have his hands roaming over her body, warming her, filling her with unimaginable pleasure.

"There's nothing wrong with you kissing me or me kissing you. You've been alone for a long, long time," he murmured. "Surely you're not feeling like you're betraying the man who was once your husband."

She tried to swallow the heavy ache in her throat. "That's not what I'm thinking," she reasoned, then shook her head. "Well, maybe I am—a little. But that's not what worries me most."

His hands slipped from her shoulders to curl around her upper arms. "There shouldn't be anything worrying you."

Turning, she rested her palms against the middle of his chest and tried to smile. "Bowie, this is all just a casual thing for you. With me—"

"Who said it was casual?" he interrupted.

She groaned. "No one has to say it. I know it. But I'm not blaming you for that. I don't expect you to think in my terms. You're too young to think in my terms."

His features were suddenly stiff and resentful. "And what sort of terms are those?"

As hot color flooded her cheeks, she started to turn away from him, but he caught her hands and held them tight.

"Please, Ava," he implored. "Don't dismiss me. It's obvious you think the only thing on my mind is sex. But that's not true. I want to know what you're thinking and why."

Ava decided it was a good thing he was holding her hands, because her knees were growing weaker by the second. If she didn't back away and put some space between their bodies, she feared she was going to melt in a pool at his feet.

"Okay. What I'm thinking is simple, Bowie. You're too young for me. Or I'm too old for you. Whichever way you want to look at it."

"I don't want to look at it from any angle. And neither should you be looking. Not when you can be feeling."

His head bent and she closed her eyes as his nose nuzzled over her cheek, up to the corner of her eye and down to the lobe of her ear.

*Oh my, oh my.* She felt like a butterfly fluttering above a bed of wildflowers as the hot sun shimmered all around her. His touch shouldn't be taking her on this much of a journey. But it was.

She instinctively drew closer to the tempting heat of his body. "I am feeling, Bowie," she whispered. "Far too much."

He didn't bother to reply. Instead, his mouth returned to hers and this time Ava couldn't fight the desire that was growing deep inside her. Without thought or hesitation, her mouth opened and invited his tongue to mate with hers. He swiftly complied and the intimate contact caused her senses to swirl at a drunken speed.

After a time she sensed his hands releasing the tight clench on hers and then his arms were sliding around her waist, enveloping her in a band of hot steel. To have him holding her, to feel his lips dancing erotically on hers, was shooting her common sense straight to outer space.

She was sliding her arms around his neck when her hand passed over a bulge of bandage beneath his shirt. The encounter was an instant reminder of who and what he was. A man nine years younger than she. A man who chose to work on the edge of danger. And most of all, a man who had no intention of settling down and making a home with any woman.

The sanity of her thoughts was enough to give her the strength to ease out of his arms and step backward until a safe distance stretched between them.

"What's wrong?" he asked, his voice gruff with desire. "Why are you looking at me like that?"

Ava didn't know how she was looking at him, but she had an idea there was a tortured expression on her face. Because right at this moment it was all she could do to keep from flinging herself back in his arms and begging him to make love to her.

What was happening to her? She was desperately trying to remember how she'd felt when Lawrence had kissed her, but try as she might, she couldn't remember feeling this much intensity. She couldn't remember the beat of her heart making such a wild chant in her ears, or the heat of her blood rushing through her, burning deep within her belly.

"I—I just remembered about your burns." Her words came out in a breathless rush and something, she didn't know what, prompted her to step back to him. "Did I hurt your shoulder?"

A faint smile touched his lips and Ava wanted to kiss him there, to taste all that joy and make it her own.

"The only way you can hurt me is by pulling away, Ava."

She lowered her eyes, staring at the toe of his cowboy boot. "I don't want to pull away from you, Bowie. But if I stay in your arms I'm not sure what might happen."

His fingers tunneled into her hair and gently stroked until the strands were lying smooth on her shoulder. The tender touch mesmerized her so much that she closed her eyes and for one sweet moment allowed herself to imagine this man making long, hot love to her.

"The normal thing that happens when a man and a woman want each other. That's what might happen."

Tilting her head back, she searched his eyes and wondered why she couldn't let herself reach for all that he was offering. She'd been empty and alone for so long. Bowie could change her life, fill it with pleasure and purpose. But for how long? What would happen once the fire between them burned out?

"That would be a huge mistake, Bowie. We'd only end up hurting each other. What we need is to…just be friends."

Beneath her hair, his fingers touched the back of her neck and moved ever so slowly over her skin. Ava could only imagine how it would feel to have his fingers sliding over her naked body, marking it with trails of fire.

"Impossible," he murmured. "I've kissed you and held you in my arms. I could never think of you as a friend. You're a desirable woman, Ava. My woman."

His woman! The image was a heady thought, but she had to push it out of her mind and fast. Being lonely wasn't nearly as bad as carrying around a broken heart. And that's exactly what Bowie Calhoun would be to any woman. A heartbreaker.

She drew in a deep breath and licked her lips. "No. I'm not your woman. And I don't plan to be. Not now or ever."

His hands slipped to the small of her back and pulled her even tighter to the front of his body.

"Then I'll just have to change your mind. Starting now. With this."

Before she could avoid the swift descent of his head, his lips were back on hers. And then resisting suddenly didn't seem to matter. Eventually, this man would break her heart. But for tonight he was giving her a glimpse of what it would be like to love again. And the image was too good to resist.

## *Chapter Six*

When Bowie hobbled down to the kitchen, Rafe was at the table drinking a cup of coffee. Next to him, Austin was sitting in a high chair, banging a spoon with loud enthusiasm on the plastic tray.

"Well, well. Look what the cat dragged in," Rafe said as he spotted Bowie. "What's brought you downstairs so early this morning, little brother?"

"Hunger. That's usually why a man shows up at the breakfast table, isn't it?"

Bowie propped his crutch to one side and sank into a chair opposite Rafe's. Immediately Austin whined and held his arms out for his uncle to rescue him from the high chair.

"Uncle Bowie isn't going to hold you," Rafe said to his son. "You need to show him how you can eat your cereal like a big boy."

For a moment, Austin's bottom lip quivered, but he didn't cry, and it was all Bowie could do to keep from getting up and plucking the kid out of the high chair. Austin was going to be a strong little guy with a mind of his own and Bowie admired that greatly.

"You eat your cereal, Austin, and then we'll go to the family room and play with your toys," Bowie promised his nephew.

Across the room, Greta poured a mug full of coffee and carried it over to Bowie, then stood back with her arms folded across her breasts.

"When will you learn that I'm not a short-order cook? You should've been down here two hours ago when I first made breakfast. What do you expect me to stir up now?"

"Well, hellfire," Bowie told her. "This morning instead of eating alone in my room I decide to hobble down the stairs to see your pretty face and this is what I get. Thanks, Greta, you're a real sweetheart."

"And you think you still got what it takes to charm a fly off the wall, but this woman ain't falling for it. You'll get what was left over from breakfast and be glad for it."

She stomped off and Bowie took a grateful sip of the coffee. Across the table, Rafe studied him with a keen eye.

"You look tired. Are your burns keeping you awake?"

Bowie grimaced even as telltale heat spread up his throat and over his jaws. "It's hard to find a way to lie comfortably. But I manage."

He wasn't about to admit to Rafe that thoughts of Ava had kept him awake most of the night. Ever since he'd left her house last night, he'd been asking himself if he'd made a huge mistake by kissing her. Not just once, but many times before the evening had ended.

Bowie hadn't planned on that happening. And he'd certainly not planned on it turning his senses upside down. Now he couldn't forget the way she'd made him feel. He'd never felt such a desperate need to make love to any woman before, but something had given him the strength to finally pull away from her. Maybe in the back of his mind, he'd been afraid to make that much of a commitment to her. Or maybe he'd had sense enough to realize she wasn't ready to make any sort of promise to him. Either way, he'd not wanted to leave her last night. And that fact alone was worrisome.

"Everything is healing okay, isn't it?"

Rafe's question interrupted Bowie's deep thoughts and he mentally shook himself before glancing over at his brother. "Sure. As far as I know. Ava tells me everything appears to be healing nicely."

"And she should know," Greta spoke up from across the room. "She made sure he got his nutrition last night by making dinner for him."

Bowie scowled at the cook. "Greta! Can't you keep that mouth of yours shut once in a while?"

Looking over her shoulder, she glared back at him. "Well, forgive me for talking. I didn't realize it was supposed to be a secret."

Letting out a huff, she turned back to the stove.

Rafe couldn't stifle a smile. "And here I was thinking your burns had kept you up all night."

Bowie sipped his coffee before he flashed a quick glance at his brother. "For your information I got home at an early hour," he said stiffly. "Ask Frank. He was my driver."

A puzzled frown creased Rafe's forehead. "I was only

kidding, Bowie. What the hell is wrong with you, anyway?"

Bowie blew out a heavy sigh. "Nothing is wrong. I'm just wondering why the two of you think my personal business is your entertainment."

Greta marched over to the table and plopped a small platter in front of him. Despite her bluster, she'd made him an omelet stuffed with cheese and jalapeños and smothered with picante sauce. Next to his right hand, she placed a silver warmer filled with flour tortillas.

Seeing how the woman had gone to extra trouble to make his breakfast made Bowie feel even worse. "Thanks, Greta. Maybe Santa will bring you something nice for Christmas this year."

"Yeah. Like getting you back on your feet and out of this house," the cook muttered, then disappeared into a connecting utility room.

Across the table Rafe smiled but said nothing as he carefully wiped milk from Austin's face.

"Where is Colleen?" Bowie asked.

"She and her mom are doing something upstairs. I think Lilly is going to take her shopping today. She wants to buy gifts for everyone on the ranch," he added wryly.

"Sounds like you're going to be spending some money today."

Rafe chuckled and Bowie could see how giving to his wife and children made his brother a happy man.

"I'm not worried. Colleen will fall asleep long before the money runs out."

Bowie dug into the omelet and the food helped lift his mood. Hopefully by the time Ava arrived he could face her as though nothing had happened between them last night. But he seriously doubted he had that much acting ability.

"I'm surprised Ava allowed you to get off the ranch. Lilly tells me she was pretty upset when she heard I'd taken you out to Antelope Range."

Bowie could've told his brother that Ava's dinner invitation had more than surprised him. He was still wondering what was behind her motive. "I've been complaining of cabin fever. And she doesn't want me getting in any nasty environments."

"Hmm. I guess her place would be cleaner than a cattle pasture and a truck with manure on the floor mats." Rafe looked over at him. "Bowie, I was joking around earlier, but I understand what this downtime must be doing to you. If I was in your situation, I'd be climbing the walls and yelling at everyone."

Bowie shrugged. "I want to get back to work. It's hell to wake up every morning and not have a purpose."

"You're talking about the hotshot crew now?"

"What else?"

Rafe casually picked up his coffee cup. "Peak season for fires in the western states is over right now," he remarked.

"That's true. But the central and southern part of the country is still in the fire danger zone. The crew might be needed at any time."

"Have you talked to any of the guys on the crew lately?"

"A few of them have called to check on me. They didn't talk much shop, though. I guess they were afraid it would only make me feel worse about being hurt and out of commission."

"Once the doctor clears you, I guess you'll have to hit the gym pretty hard to get back in working shape."

"I can't wait."

Rafe didn't say anything and for long moments the only sound in the kitchen was Austin slurping milk from his cereal bowl.

"You know," he finally said, "the Silver Horn has thousands of acres, thousands of cows and hundreds of horses. If you followed me around every day you wouldn't have time to get bored."

Bowie let out a mocking grunt. "You'd get tired of having to lead me around."

"Lead you around? Ha. Being a cowboy was ingrained in you long before you ever donned a military uniform. You've not forgotten anything about ranching. You just want everyone else to believe you have."

"You don't get it, Rafe. I want to be the best at what I do. I don't want to just get by."

Rafe shot him a knowing grin. "In other words, you want to ride point instead of drag. Well, you always liked a challenge. When you get healthy again, you can prove you're worthy of that position."

Bowie started to tell Rafe that whenever he got healthy again, he was heading straight back to the hotshot crew. But before he had the chance to say anything, Rafe's phone jingled with a text message.

After quickly scanning the message, Rafe said, "Denver needs me at the cattle barn. Some sort of emergency. I need to get gone. Would you tell Greta to take Austin back upstairs to his mother?"

"Don't worry about Austin. I'm going to take him to the family room with me."

Rafe chuckled as he tugged on his Stetson and grabbed

a heavy coat off the back of his chair. "You keeping company with a baby. You must be getting desperate."

"Austin is a perfect partner," Bowie said to Rafe's retreating back. "He doesn't talk back."

Ava hurried up the walkway to the Silver Horn ranch house, a fierce north wind whipping snow straight into her face. Glad that she'd broken habit this morning and dressed in white pants and warm lined boots, she clutched the hood of her coat close to her throat and knocked on the kitchen door.

Greta immediately swung the door wide. "Get in here, girl, before you freeze!" she exclaimed.

Ava stomped the snow from her boots and hurried into the warm kitchen. The scents of bacon and chorizo sausage lingered in the air, reminding Ava she'd not taken time to eat breakfast this morning.

"The weather is definitely turning nasty," Ava told the cook. "The closer I came to the ranch, the worse it got."

While she hung her coat on a nearby hall tree, Greta said, "Bowie came down for breakfast this morning."

"Oh. That's good."

"Humph. You might call it good. I'd just as soon he stayed in his room."

Deciding it best not to dig into the woman's remarks, she asked, "Do you know if he's in his room now?"

"Tessa just took him coffee in the family room. You should find him there."

"Thanks."

She started out of the room, but Greta's voice caused her to pause and look back.

"Miss Archer, you take a real close look at that boy this morning. There's something wrong with him."

Alarmed, Ava asked, "Wrong? Is he feeling sick?"

"No! He's as mean as an old bear."

"Oh. Well, I hate to disappoint you, Greta, but I don't have much control over Bowie's moods."

"I wouldn't sell myself short," she said, then turned back to the counter where a mound of yeast dough was waiting to be kneaded.

Ava wasn't exactly sure what Greta was getting at. But if the woman was thinking she had some sort of romantic hold over Bowie, she was mistaken. Bowie might have enjoyed kissing her last night, but she was hardly important to his moods or anything else about his life.

"I'll go find him," she told Greta and left the kitchen.

As she made her way through the house, she noticed the Christmas decorations, but thoughts about the upcoming holiday couldn't distract her one-track mind. Ever since she'd climbed out of bed this morning, she'd been wondering how to greet the man. What could he possibly be thinking about her after the way she'd kissed him so passionately? If he'd not had the sense to end things and call for his ride, she very well might have invited him into her bed.

*Don't think about that now. Just think about caring for Bowie's medical needs and maybe the urge to make love to him will die a natural death.*

When Ava first stepped into the family room, she didn't see anyone. And then she heard a low male voice singing what sounded to her like a cowboy lullaby. She couldn't hear all the words, but as she stepped farther into the room, she picked up something about a tumbleweed and a buckaroo.

And then she spotted the large wooden rocker facing

a wall of paned windows. Bowie had Austin cradled in his arms and the baby appeared to be sound asleep.

The sight brought a lump of emotion to Ava's throat and for long moments, she stood there staring at the man and child, wondering why Bowie looked so perfect in the fatherly scene. He was a man who craved adventure, not a family.

Forcing herself to let her presence be known, she walked over to the rocker. Bowie immediately looked up and smiled. And suddenly the awkwardness about seeing him again dissolved beneath the happy flutter of her heart.

"I think the little guy is down for the count," he said.

"That's the quietest I've ever seen him," Ava admitted with a smile. "Where's Lilly?"

"Christmas shopping. I'll have to get Tessa to take Austin upstairs."

"No hurry. I'm a little early this morning anyway," she told him. "Since it's snowing again, I thought I'd give myself extra driving time."

He motioned to a burgundy leather armchair to his left. "Help yourself to coffee and have a seat. I'll call Tessa."

He picked up his cell phone and typed a message. When he placed it back on the table next to him, Ava asked, "You text the maid? I thought the Silver Horn had an intercom system."

He grinned impishly. "Tessa and I have a secret code."

"In other words, she spoils you."

"Well, I am nonambulatory."

And completely charming, Ava thought. She doubted he'd ever met a woman he couldn't wrap around his finger. And last night she'd been equally guilty of succumbing to his charisma. The realization made the commonsense part of her feel foolish, but the feminine part of her didn't feel that way at all. It felt excited and wanted and terribly alive.

She poured herself a cup of coffee from the silver thermos on the lamp table and after adding a dollop of cream, she took a seat in the armchair.

"I never would've guessed you knew how to rock a baby," she said. "You didn't learn that in the Marines, did you?"

A wan smile touched his face. "Didn't learn it on the hotshot crew, either."

She studied him over the rim of her cup. "Where did you learn it?"

He slanted her a wry look. "In case you haven't noticed, my brothers and sister have been having babies right and left. Once I got back here to the Silver Horn, I figured out Uncle Bowie had to learn real quick how to deal with kids."

Ava wanted to tell him he looked like a natural. But she kept the thought to herself. The last thing she wanted was for him to think she had babies and home and hearth on her mind. Especially where he was concerned.

His gaze swept over her and Ava suddenly felt as though she was back in his arms with his lips caressing hers, his body filling hers with heat.

"You wore pants today."

She nodded. "The wind is brutal this morning."

He started to say something else, but a slight noise at the opposite end of the room had both of them glancing around to see Tessa walking toward them.

The young maid smiled a greeting at Ava, then went

straight to Bowie. "I'll take Mr. Austin off your hands," she told him. "Is there anything else you need?"

"How about a new ankle?" he teased.

Tessa pulled a playful face at him. "You better ask Santa for one of those."

Once she'd lifted Austin into her arms and disappeared from the room, Ava looked over at him.

"Have you ever thought that Tessa is much more suited for you than I am?"

His eyes widened a fraction and then he laughed. "That's funny, Ava. Tessa is young and pretty, but she's like a little sister. You see, she's been here with the family since she was about fourteen—or something like that. I can't remember exactly."

Ava frowned. "Surely she didn't come here to work at that age? What about her parents and school?"

"As far as I know, she only had a mother. And she died in a car accident. My mother was good friends with Tessa's mother. I guess that's why Dad felt inclined to take Tessa in. Because he knew that Mom wouldn't have hesitated to give the girl a home. Dad never intended for her to become a maid, but once she got old enough, Tessa saw the job as a way to thank the Calhoun family for giving her a home. For the past couple of years she's been taking college courses online. She wants to get a degree in criminal justice."

"It's nice that she has such ambition. What about her father?"

Bowie frowned. "Tessa never knew him. From what she says, he left long before she was born."

There had been plenty of times Ava had bemoaned the fact that her parents were divorced and their home was technically broken. Yet hearing Tessa's story made her realize how fortunate she was to have a father and to know that he loved her.

"What made you say that about me and Tessa?"

Lowering her coffee cup, she looked at him. "I guess in the light of day I can see things more clearly."

"Does that mean last night you weren't seeing clearly?"

Her heart thudded faster. "Were you? You left in rather a hurry," she dared to say. "I'm not sure what you were thinking—or feeling."

He slanted her a look that was both guilty and beseeching. "I'm sorry, Ava. I'll tell you exactly what I was thinking—that if I stayed a minute longer, we were going to wind up in bed. And I wasn't sure you were ready for that. I wasn't even sure I was ready."

Her face flaming with heat, she rose to her feet and walked over to the windows. Beyond the glass was a wintry view of the backyard and farther beyond, the snow-capped mountains to the west. But her mind was only registering part of the beautiful scene. Instead, she was seeing Bowie's face, feeling his mouth against hers, his hands awakening places in her body that had lain dead for so many years.

"I didn't think men had much of a conscience when it came to sex," she said flatly.

"This man does."

The conviction in his voice had her turning to look at him. "So you decided last night that I'm not what you want?"

A stunned expression passed over his features and then he reached for his crutch. Ava waited for him to cross the short space between them and as she did, her heart thudded with a dread she didn't understand.

All along she'd been telling herself that she couldn't

let her feelings for this man deepen. All along she'd been doing her best to convince him and herself that they had no business having any sort of romantic relationship. Yet at this very moment it was dawning on her just exactly how much he was becoming a part of her life.

He stood in front of her and as his gaze met hers, his features softened. "Ava, you're way off base," he said gently. "I still want you just as much. Maybe even more."

The need to touch him had her reaching for his hand, and he complied by wrapping his fingers around hers.

Shaking her head, she gazed down at their feet. "I'm confused, Bowie. About myself. You. Us. Last night, for the first time in years, you made me feel like a woman. And I—I wanted you to make love to me."

He lifted her chin and then his fingertips were tracing a tender trail across her cheek. "I don't want you to have regrets, Ava. If I ever saw that on your face it would crush me."

What was he saying? That her feelings actually mattered to him? The notion rattled her so much, she couldn't form a single word.

And then the moment was lost as a vacuum cleaner suddenly sounded just outside the room.

"We—uh—shouldn't be talking about this here," she finally managed to whisper. "Your family might walk in at any minute. Besides, last night is over."

"But we aren't." He wrapped a hand around her upper arm and urged her away from the windows. "Let's go up to my room. We'll finish this while you're dressing my burns."

She followed his slow progress out of the room, but once they reached the staircase, he insisted she go before him.

"I've wished a thousand times that I'd been on the stairs with my mother when she took that misstep," he said. "I could've caught her. Or at least broken her fall."

He wanted to protect her, Ava realized as she slowly climbed the wide staircase to the second floor. Even in his compromised condition, he was willing to sacrifice his well-being for hers. That alone melted her heart like nothing else.

"It wasn't meant to happen that way, Bowie." Glancing over her shoulder, she gave him a faint smile. "But I'm always careful on the stairs. I promise."

By the time Bowie got to his room, he was weak and out of breath, a fact that made him angry. He'd always been fit and strong, and to be so vulnerable, especially in front of Ava, crushed his ego.

When he finally reached the side of the bed, he wanted to fling the crutch to the far side of the room, but he stopped himself. He was already having enough trouble proving he was mature enough to be her partner. Behaving like a pouting child certainly wouldn't help his cause.

"Sit down, Bowie, and I'll get my things."

He blew out a long breath. "I think I'd better. I feel as weak as a newborn kitten."

She must have detected the frustration in his voice because she suddenly turned back to him, a look of concern on her face.

"That will change. Especially when your cast comes off and you can begin to move around more."

"Yeah. I know. I need to be patient. But I'm not cut out for patience."

A faint smile curved her lips as she walked toward him, and Bowie's thoughts were quickly distracted as he took in the full curves of her breasts beneath the thin white sweater, the indention of her waist and the tempting flare of her hips. When he'd held her in his arms last night, he'd felt all that warmth and softness against him and the need for more had left him aching.

"You must have patience," she said. "You managed to get Austin to fall asleep."

The closer she got the more shallow his breathing grew. No woman had ever had this much effect on him. Even if he wasn't burned or broken, he knew he'd still feel helpless in her presence. And that was a sobering thought.

"That didn't require patience. The little guy likes me."

"I like you, too," she said softly.

By now she was standing in front of him and when her hand gently cupped the side of his face, he couldn't bear it. Before he could stop himself, he snatched a hold of her wrist and tugged her down on the bed beside him.

The unexpected motion caused both of them to topple over onto the mattress.

Bowie suddenly found his face next to hers and though he wanted to kiss her ripe lips, he hesitated as a myriad of emotions poured through him.

"You shouldn't be lying on your side," she murmured softly.

His gaze remained locked on hers as his fingers found the pins in her hair and pulled them from the heavy twist. Once the silky waves fell around her shoulders, he wound a strand around his fingers and leaned his forehead against hers.

"I shouldn't be doing a lot of things. But I can't keep my hands off you, Ava. I want like hell to be well again. I want to make love to you and when I do I don't want either of us to be thinking about my burns, my ankle or anything else."

"Is that why you left last night?"

He eased his head back, then groaned at the doubts he saw in her eyes.

"Not exactly. Down in the family room I was trying to tell you that this thing between us… It's much more for me than just touching you."

That was more than he'd ever said to any woman, and though it would've scared him to make such an admission before, it didn't now. Instead, it felt as though something hidden deep inside him had broken free, and the release was almost euphoric.

"And what could that mean to you in the days and weeks to come?" she asked.

With a troubled sigh, she eased away from him and rose from the bed. Bowie sat on the edge of the mattress and watched her walk over and stare pensively out the window.

"I don't know," he admitted. "Nor do I know what it might mean to you. But I think we owe it to each other to find out."

She glanced over at him and as Bowie looked at her, he realized that even when her dark hair was threaded with gray, even when wrinkles touched the corners of her eyes, she would still be beautiful and sexy to him. He didn't understand how a man of his age could see the future with such clarity. But then, he wasn't exactly looking at Ava with his eyes. He was looking at her with his heart.

"You want to get well and I want that for you. Very much. But I dread the day." She looked away from him and swallowed. "Because when that day comes, our time together will be over."

He started to get up and go to her, but before he could, she returned and with a stoic expression, began to undo the buttons on his shirt.

"You're wrong, Ava."

She kept her gaze on the middle of his chest. "It's time I changed your bandages and headed back to town. And when I leave, I don't want to feel sad and lonely. Let's talk about something else."

"Like what?"

"Christmas is coming. Are you going to buy gifts for your family?"

He didn't want to talk about presents. He wanted to convince her they had more than a few weeks together. But he knew she wasn't ready for that, so he went along with her diversion. "I always buy gifts for my family," he replied. "Will you take me shopping?"

She pushed his shirt off his shoulders and the touch of her fingers against his bare skin sent a zing of heat radiating down his arm.

"It wouldn't be wise for you to be out in crowded places. Not until your burns are more healed. If you caught the flu or picked up a bug of some sort, you'd be in trouble."

The scent of her hair and skin was doing crazy things to his senses, making it a struggle to keep his mind on their conversation.

"Looks like I'll have to do my shopping online, then. What are you going to get me for Christmas?"

She cast a skeptical glance at him. "What could I possibly get for a man who already has everything?"

He grinned. "Not everything, Ava."

"Then make me a list and I'll see if I can afford anything on it," she said with a shake of her head.

"Money has nothing to do with it. Or me. Or Christmas."

Her soft laugh was full of cynicism. "And you expect me to believe that?"

The smile on his face deepened as he reached for her hand and lifted the back of it to his lips. "Before the holiday is over, sweet Ava, I'll have you believing in Christmas angels, Santa Claus and me."

## Chapter Seven

For the next two days the ER was bombarded with cases of flu and frostbite, along with broken bones and sprains due to falls on the ice and snow. By Friday night, the last night of her workweek, she was looking forward to an evening off. Especially since Bowie had invited her to a Christmas party being given for the ranch hands.

"I've never heard so much coughing in my life. And why do people wait until night to decide they need emergency care? Haven't they heard of medical clinics?"

Ava looked up from the clipboard in her hand to see Paige entering the nurse's station. Her friend looked exhausted to the point of being sick herself.

"Are you all right?" Ava asked. "You're not coming down with the flu, are you?"

Paige's head swung back and forth as she dropped her tall frame onto a padded stool. "I hope not. I think I just need twenty-four hours of nonstop sleep. Unfortunately that isn't going to happen. I'm meeting Mom at the mall bright and early in the morning. She has this idea that she can't do her Christmas shopping without me."

Ava slipped the clipboard into a holder at the end of the countertop, then turned to her friend. "Are you scheduled for tomorrow night's shift?"

She let out a weary groan. "Yes. What about you?"

"No."

"Lucky you. I don't expect you're going to spend your downtime visiting dozens of stores and standing in checkout lines to pay for gifts that nobody wants. You don't have anyone to buy gifts for," she said, then suddenly realizing how that sounded, she pressed fingers over her lips. "Oh. Sorry, Ava. I didn't mean that the way it sounded. I just meant that you don't have a bunch of brothers or sisters and all their kids."

Ava leveled a pointed look at her friend. "Why not say the rest? That I don't have a husband or babies of my own?"

Paige grimaced. "Because I don't have a husband or babies, either. After having a cheating husband and now watching my sister deal with that miserable husband of hers, I'm not sure I'd ever want to marry again. Even if Mr. Dreamy walked right into this nurses' station and swept me off my feet."

"Nurse Winters! Do you think you can get off that can of yours and give me some assistance?"

The sarcastic male voice caused all five nurses to look toward an open doorway. Dr. Sherman was boring a hole through Paige, as though she was the only nurse milling behind the work counter.

Fire flashed in Paige's gray eyes, but she didn't retort.

Once the doctor disappeared from the doorway, though, she rolled her eyes at Ava as she slid off the stool.

"Merry Christmas," she muttered. "I'd better go find Dr. Scrooge."

As Paige hurried away, the head nurse of the evening ER shift, a stout woman with short iron-gray hair, walked up beside Ava.

"Looks like Dr. Sherman has finally met his match," the older nurse observed. "He likes her."

Ava frowned. "What are you talking about, Helen? Dr. Sherman picks on Paige all the time. She ought to give him a piece of her mind."

"You shouldn't talk that way, Ava. The man has been hurt."

Unmoved, Ava replied, "So what? We've all gone through pain and disappointment. Some of us just handle it better than others."

Helen cocked a pointed brow at Ava. "I guess you think you've handled it well?"

For a moment the question took Ava aback and then she felt a sheepish look come over her face. Had she been guilty of rubbing her despair onto everyone around her?

Helen was still waiting for Ava's answer when one of the phones rang and she answered it.

At the same moment, the swinging doors to the treatment room suddenly burst open and two medics pushed in a gurney carrying a child.

Instantly, everything fled from her mind, and Ava hurried over to the child, nothing as important as caring for her patient.

Ava was ready and waiting when Bowie arrived to take her to the Silver Horn Christmas party. As soon as she spotted the ranch truck pulling into the driveway, she locked the door behind her and hurried out to the vehicle.

By the time she reached it, an older man with a wide-brimmed cowboy hat and a face full of wrinkles stepped down from the driver's door to greet her.

"Hello, ma'am. I'm Frank. I'll be driving you and Mr. Bowie tonight."

She offered the man her hand. "Thank you, Frank. I appreciate you coming to get me."

"My pleasure," he assured her.

At that moment, the rear passenger door opened and Bowie called to her. "Back here, Ava. I'd get down and help you in, but we'd be here awhile."

"I'll help the lady in," Frank told him.

The cowboy kindly gave her a hand up into the truck, then took his place behind the wheel. Since Bowie was sitting in the middle of the backseat, she had no choice but to snuggle close to his side. He promptly buckled the seat belt across her lap.

"Wow, you look beautiful tonight." He grinned, appreciation lighting his eyes. "Don't you think she looks beautiful, Frank?"

"Like a cactus rose covered in morning dew," the old man agreed as he maneuvered the truck down a quiet residential street.

Bowie chuckled at his response. "Frank considers himself a poet. About a hundred years ago, he came up here from Texas to work on the Silver Horn. He still says the ranch is small compared to Texas standards."

Frank laughed. "You're full of it, you young sprout. Now pay attention to your girl and leave me to drive."

"That will be very easy." Bending his head close to

Ava's, Bowie folded her small hand beneath his large one. "Are you looking forward to the party?"

"Yes. We have a bit of an office party at the hospital during the Christmas season, but this is the first real party I've been to in a long, long time."

"Well, I'm a little bummed," he admitted. "Because I can't dance with this cast on my foot. But everything else will be fun."

"Oh," she said with surprise. "There will be dancing? I thought this was going to be just a food and talking thing."

His smile was patient. "When the Calhouns throw a shindig, we don't hold back. There'll be music and dancing, food and drinks, gifts and games." He glanced impishly toward the front seat. "Frank is all about enjoying the spiked punch. He's too old for dancing."

"When you get that cast off, boy, you'd better run, because I'm gonna be after you. And once I catch you, it won't be pretty."

Frank's threat brought a happy laugh from Bowie, and Ava glanced from one man to the other. The exchange between them intrigued her. Bowie had never come off like a snob to her, yet it was obvious he was close to this man, which surprised her. Frank was clearly a ranch hand and from the remarks that Bowie often made, he wanted nothing to do with being a part of the cowboy life. The whole thing made her wonder if there was a portion of him that was more bound to the ranch than he realized. Yet even if he was, even if he did want to make the ranch his life's work, would that close the gap of differences between them?

One glance over at his handsome profile told her she

didn't want to try to answer those questions tonight. This evening was going to be all about having fun with Bowie.

She wished Helen could see her now. The older nurse would probably cluck her tongue and say, "It's about time, Ava."

The Christmas party for the ranch hands was being held in a huge hay barn located next to the cattle pens. Ava had expected the inside of the building to be crude with dirt floors and dusty walls. Instead, the enormous area had been cleaned down to a wood-plank floor. At one end, a huge spruce tree glittered with twinkling lights and decorations. Beneath it, festively wrapped gifts were piled all the way to the lower branches. More twinkling lights and tinsel hung from the rafters, while around the barn, poinsettias and Norwegian firs accented bales of hay serving as benches. On the opposite end from the Christmas tree, a small wooden platform held a four-piece band that included a guitar, a stand-up bass, drums and a fiddle.

As Bowie ushered Ava over to one of the hay bales, the ensemble was playing a holiday tune. Some of the cowboys, with drinks in hand, had gathered close to the band, enthusiastically singing backup for the guitar player.

"They sound good," Ava observed.

Bowie laughed. "Just wait till the night wears on. There'll be a bunch of whoops and hollers mixed in with all that singing."

Ava chuckled. "I'll take your word for it."

Before they took a seat, he gestured toward an area where long tables were set up with food and refreshment. "I'd say I would get you a drink, but with this crutch I'd probably spill most of it before I got back here. Would you like something? I think Dad hired servers. I'll try to catch the attention of one."

He'd hardly gotten the words out of his mouth when Rafe and Lilly walked up to them.

Lilly smacked a kiss on Ava's cheek. "Merry Christmas, dear friend. You look great tonight."

Ava hadn't been sure about wearing jeans, boots and an emerald-green sweater to the party, but now that she was seeing the other women in similar clothing, she was glad she'd dressed casually.

"Thanks. So do you." Her gaze took in both Lilly and Rafe. "Where are the kids?"

"Poor Tessa is up in the nursery caring for all the Calhoun babies."

"You mean she won't get to attend the party?" Ava asked with dismay. "She works so hard. I'm sure she needs a break."

Lilly said, "We tried, Ava. I already had a sitter lined up to deal with the kids, but Tessa wouldn't hear of it."

"She's not the partying type," Rafe said, then gave Bowie a sly wink. "Not like my little brother here."

Bowie groaned. "Oh, sure. In my shape I can really kick up my heels."

"Once the doctors pronounce you fit, you'll be painting the town again with all your hotshot buddies."

Bowie scowled at him. "You talk too much, Rafe."

The other man laughed before glancing coyly at Ava. "Well, you don't need to worry about Ava. There are plenty of guys around tonight who'll be more than glad to waltz her around the dance floor."

Bowie glanced behind him where extra hay was stacked to the ceiling. "Uh, do you think any old bullwhips are lying around here?"

Laughing, Rafe slapped the middle of Bowie's chest before curling an arm around his wife's waist. "Come on, honey, let's go get something to drink."

Lilly gave them a departing wave while Bowie looked at Ava and groaned.

"I apologize, Ava."

"For what? Because Rafe and Lilly assumed we're more than nurse and patient?"

She was surprised to see red color wash over his face. For a man who was supposedly a playboy, she thought, he blushed at the simplest things. And that alone was enough to charm her.

"No. Because you had to put up with their teasing."

Ava laughed softly. "I've been friends with Lilly a long time, and after she married Rafe, he became a friend, too. I'd think something was wrong if the two of them weren't doing a little joking."

He looked relieved. "Good. Then maybe you won't get offended by the rest of the family."

By the time the party got into full swing, all of Bowie's family had stopped by to say hello. For the first time Ava met Bowie's eldest brother, Clancy, and his wife, Olivia. As general manager of the Silver Horn, the tall cowboy appeared to be much more reserved than Bowie and Rafe. He was cordial and warm and Ava was particularly touched by the loving looks he bestowed upon his pretty wife. As for Bowie's father, she'd already met him a few times before, but she'd not been introduced to his girlfriend, Noreen, until this evening. The attractive dark-haired DA was much younger than Orin, yet the span of years between them hardly seemed to be an issue with anyone—a fact that helped Ava not feel so conspicuous about the age gap between her and Bowie.

Later on, Evan and his wife, Noelle, took time off the dance floor to spend a few minutes with Ava and Bowie. And then their sister, Sassy, and her husband, Jett, had waltzed by to say hello. By then a meal of barbecued beef and all the trimmings was ready to eat and everyone made their way over to a group of tables to partake of the buffet.

Once the meal was over, the drinks began to flow at a steady pace. As Bowie had predicted, the whooping and hollering began, along with much more dancing. Several men approached Ava to take a whirl around the floor, but she declined. There was no way she was going to leave Bowie sitting with a cast on his foot.

Eventually, some of the guys pulled out a roping dummy shaped like a steer, along with a bucking barrel, and the fun and games began. After one man was crowned the roping champion and another the best rough stock rider, Orin announced it was time for the gifts to be handed out.

Ava was surprised that everyone at the party received a gift, but she was even more stunned when she discovered they were all personalized.

"Who does all of this?" she asked Bowie. "There must be at least seventy-five people here!"

A clever smile spread over his features. "Frank told me Santa Claus and his reindeer came through the ranch yard last night. He must have delivered everything to the barn."

"Sure. And how did Santa know this was my favorite perfume?" She held up a small bottle of the floral scent.

Chuckling, he said, "Christmas is magic. Eventually you're going to start believing."

Across the way, the band began playing "White Christmas." Bowie reached for her hand. "Let's dance," he said.

"Your cast. How—"

Before she could finish, he rose and tugged her up from the hay bale. "I can stand. And we can pretend. So humor me, okay?"

Even though she'd been sitting close to his side all evening, the urge to be even closer was impossible to resist. With a saucy smile, she stepped into his arms and, wrapping her hand in his, he began to sway her back and forth in time to the music.

"Now this is nice," he murmured against her ear. "Very nice."

Resting her cheek against his chest, she closed her eyes and let herself dream of how it would be to always have Bowie's strong arms to hold her, to wake up each morning and see his face next to hers.

"I'm glad you invited me to the party tonight, Bowie."

His fingers stroked her hair and Ava wondered if anyone was watching the two of them. Earlier this evening, he'd introduced her as his nurse, but she doubted there was a person present who connected her to Bowie in that way. Not with him cuddling her to his side the whole evening.

Funny how that didn't matter to Ava. For all these years she'd not wanted to appear linked to any man other than her late husband. Because she'd been stuck in the past and clinging to memories, she realized. Somehow Bowie had pulled her into the present and she wanted—needed—to stay there.

He murmured next to her ear, "You've made this evening very special for me."

The music continued to drift around them, while the heat of his body seeped into hers and clouded her senses with foggy pleasure. She could have stayed in his arms forever, but the song eventually ended and the band broke into an up-tempo number.

Easing a step back, she glanced ruefully at her watch. "I hate to say this, but I need to head home pretty soon. By the time someone drives me back to Carson City it will be very late."

Bowie glanced out at the crowd, his gaze surveying the merrymaking that was still going as strong as ever.

"I hadn't brought this up, Ava, but I don't think Frank, or anyone else for that matter, should be driving."

Dismay parted Ava's lips. Everyone, including herself, had been enjoying cocktails and spiked punch. The notion of needing a designated driver to take her back to Carson City had never entered her mind. Apparently it hadn't crossed Bowie's, either. Until now.

"I hadn't thought about the trip back to town," she admitted.

"Me neither. But to be honest, even if I had thought about it, I wouldn't have told Frank or anyone else to keep away from the alcohol tonight. This party only happens once a year and the men work so hard they deserve to let loose and enjoy themselves."

She turned a rueful look on him. "Looks like I'll have to call a taxi."

"Not on your life! You'll stay here on the ranch and someone will drive you home in the morning."

"Stay here? But Bowie, I'm not prepared for that. And your family—"

"You won't need a thing and my family will be glad you stayed."

Before she could put up any more protest, Bowie pulled out his cell phone and punched a number. After a moment she could tell he was speaking with Tessa.

"Yeah. That one," he said. "Great. We'll be over in a few minutes."

He put the phone away and reached for her arm. "Come on. Dad's sitting not far from the door. I'll tell him we're leaving. Unless you'd rather stay and party on?"

"Oh, no. I'm ready," she assured him. "Besides, you need to elevate your ankle. It's probably as big as a balloon."

She glanced up to see a wide grin on his face. "Always my little nurse."

"Someone has to make sure you take care of yourself."

He chuckled. "And to think I wanted the ranch vet to keep an eye on me."

A few minutes later, on the second floor, Bowie showed her into a bedroom directly next to his. "If you need for Tessa to get you anything, just lift the phone and punch the in-house line."

As Ava gazed around the opulent room, Bowie turned to go, prompting her to ask, "Are you going to bed now?"

"As soon as I get ready."

Puzzled at his abrupt departure, she watched his retreating back as he quietly shut the door behind him. She'd not expected their evening to end so suddenly, but it was getting late, she reasoned, and the day had been a long one.

Walking over to the queen-size bed, she stared in amazement. The linens had already been turned back and at the foot, an assortment of nightclothes was laid out on the rose-colored comforter. A long white satin gown with a plunging neckline edged with French lace was partnered with a matching robe. Or if she wasn't feeling that sexy, she could choose to wear a pair of silk pajamas in pale pink, coupled with a pink fleece robe. A pair of fuzzy white mules was positioned neatly on the floor next to the bed skirt.

Being a nurse, Ava was used to tending to her patients' needs. She was certainly not accustomed to having her needs cared for, especially in such a lavish way. Unlike Bowie. He had been born into wealth; he'd grown up in these surroundings. She shook her head as a thought struck her—he'd given all this up for a cot in a military barracks. Clearly the allure of danger and excitement had been undeniable.

Trying not to let that thought spoil what had so far been a wonderful evening, she went to the bathroom and brushed her teeth, then cleaned the makeup from her face, grateful for the array of bath products.

Back in the bedroom, she turned on a bedside lamp and switched off the overhead light before she returned to the bedside. She was fingering the lace on the gown, trying to decide if she wanted to wear it or the pajamas when she heard the door open behind her.

Glancing over her shoulder, she watched in fascination as Bowie, minus his crutch and wearing nothing but a pair of pajama bottoms tied low on his waist, hobbled into the room.

"If you want my opinion, I'd choose the gown." He came to a stop just behind her and curved his hands over her shoulders. "Or maybe you'd rather wear nothing at all."

His husky suggestion, coupled with the touch of his hands, sent her heart into a wild gallop. She turned to see he was studying her with heated eyes and suddenly her breathing was in a desperate race to keep up with the frantic pace of her heart.

"What are you doing in here?" she asked bluntly.

His fingertips touched her cheek and then moved on to her lower lip. Ava's knees grew so weak she feared she was going to collapse to the floor.

"I'm going to rest my ankle," he murmured. "Right next to yours."

The realization of what he was saying had her peeping around his shoulder to the door. "Your family—"

"I've locked the door," he assured her. "Besides, we're the only ones on this side of the house. No one will bother us."

Ava hesitated as all sorts of thoughts came crashing in on her. After what he'd said yesterday, she'd thought he'd nixed the idea of having sex with her. Clearly, she'd thought wrong.

"Bowie, what if—"

"No *what if*s," he interrupted. "No regrets for either of us. Okay?"

Tilting her head back, she met his gaze and the warmth and certainty she found in his green eyes filled the holes of her heart.

"I've spent the past thirteen years hanging on to *what if*s and regrets. I want to let them go, Bowie. Now. Tonight. With you."

"Ava. Sweet Ava."

Something hot and reckless flashed in his eyes and then his lips were on hers, searching, giving, taking. As he drew her closer, she placed her hands on his bare chest and the heat of his skin sizzled beneath her fingertips. Mindful of his bandages, she moved her hands over him, touching him everywhere she could without causing him pain. But after a few moments the limited exploration of her fingers wasn't enough to satisfy her. Or him.

Tearing his lips from hers, he reached for the hem of her sweater. Ava held up her arms and allowed him to pull the garment over her head. He tossed it to the floor, his eyes never leaving her breasts encased in black lace. With a groan of pleasure, his head dipped to the exposed cleavage.

Ava's breath caught in her throat as his lips touched her sensitive flesh, his tongue smoothing over her heated skin. Streaks of desire burned their way through every cell of her body, setting off an instant combustion in the deepest part of her.

Before she could shove the straps of the bra off her shoulders, he unclasped the back and lifted the scrap of material away. With her firm breasts cupped in each hand, he pulled one budded nipple into his mouth and gently sucked.

The incredible sensation caused a groan to erupt from deep within her throat.

Bowie looked up and anxiously scanned her face.

"Am I hurting you?"

"Not at all," she said in a voice choked with emotion. "I want you. So much."

A wicked smile exposed his teeth and then his mouth was back on her breasts, his tongue laving and teasing until she was arching toward him and burying her fingers into his thick hair.

How could she have forgotten this? The question raced through her mind as wave after wave of pleasure shivered through her body. Or had she ever really felt this much passion, this out-of-control feeling that was gripping her body, filling her with a need so great it was actually painful?

Her breaths had turned to raspy pants and her senses were so scattered she hardly registered the fact that they were both still standing. Until he reached for the zipper on her jeans.

"My boots," she whispered. "They have to come off before my jeans."

He nudged her onto the bed. "I'll do it."

As she lay back, he removed her boots and jeans. When he finally began to ease the black lace panties down her thighs, he shot her a naughty grin.

"And here I was thinking you wore white cotton."

"You did?"

His low chuckle was as sexy as the hank of tawny hair falling over his right eye.

"No. I'm teasing. This is how I imagined you—sexy and beautiful. Only you look even better than what I'd pictured in my head."

To have a man his age consider her beautiful and sexy was hard for her to believe, yet the glow in his eyes as he stretched out next to her was completely convincing, and it filled her with all kinds of confidence.

"If you keep looking at me like that," she whispered, "I can't be responsible for what I might do to you."

A grin curved his lips. "I can't wait, baby."

She turned to him until her breasts were flattened against his chest and her hips aligned with his. When his arm moved around her back and drew her even closer, she felt safe and protected, yet at the same time wildly tempted.

"I want to put my arm around you," she said against the warm skin of his neck. "But I can't touch your side. Or your shoulder."

"Don't worry about it. There are plenty of other places you can touch me."

She reached up and pushed her fingers through his hair. The thick wave fell across his forehead and made his features appear even younger. For one split second Ava wondered if she'd lost her mind for giving in to her desire for this man. But just as quickly the gentle, loving look in his eyes drew her thoughts and emotions straight back to him. And she knew there was no turning back. Not for her.

"That's true. But we're going to have to be very careful doing this."

A corner of his lips twitched with something like humor and then his expression turned serious. "Why? Because it's something you've not done in a long time?"

"Thirteen years is more than a long time, Bowie," she said, her voice husky with undisguised emotion. "It's a lifetime ago."

Several long moments passed in silence and then his lips pressed softly, tenderly against her forehead. "That means you're starting all over with me. And it means I don't want to disappoint you."

Just the idea that he might worry about such a thing softened her heart and had her clasping his face between her hands.

"Oh, Bowie, you couldn't."

His lips took on a wry slant. "You seem to forget I'm handicapped."

Laughing softly, she began to nibble on the side of his neck. "This isn't a boxing match."

"Maybe not, but you've already knocked me for a loop."

With that he found her mouth again and Ava groaned with pleasure as his kiss pushed her to a deep, hot place where release could only be found with his body connected to hers.

By the time he lifted his lips from hers and turned his attention to other parts of her body, she was gripped with desire and desperate to have him inside her.

When her hand slipped inside the waistband of his pajamas and wrapped around his hard shaft, she heard the sharp intake of his breath and then he was looking deep into her eyes.

"This might sound stupid, Ava, but—are you ready for this? I mean, really ready?"

She searched his face. "If you're talking about birth control—"

"No," he interrupted. "I have protection with me. I'm not talking about that. I'm talking about you and tomorrow. Like I said before, I don't want to see regret on your face."

As if she could turn back now, with her body aching for his. She'd always thought of herself as a strong woman, but she wasn't that strong. And for once in her life she didn't want to be tough and resistant. She wanted him to open the deepest part of her and take everything he wanted.

"No regrets," she whispered fiercely. "Just make love to me."

He eased off the bed and hastily removed his pajamas. Once they were out of the way, he turned his back to her and after a moment, she heard the faint rustle. He was preparing himself, she realized, and the mere thought of him sliding into her was enough to make her wet and wanting.

When he turned back to her, she opened her arms to him and as he settled into them, it dawned on her that she'd opened her heart to him, too.

## Chapter Eight

Bowie wasn't sure how or why Ava had finally invited him into her bed. Not that it mattered. From the very first moment he'd laid eyes on her, he'd fantasized about what it would be like to have sex with her. And then he'd begun to calculate just how long and hard he'd have to court her before she'd surrender to him.

But now that he was lying next to her and she was kissing him so sweetly and wantonly, something deep within him recognized that this was so much more than sex. He wanted her. Oh, yes, more than he'd ever wanted any woman. But his feelings didn't stop there. Everything about her, from the sound of her sigh to the erotic dance of her fingertips against his skin and the wild taste of her lips, was being burned into his brain, and he knew without a doubt these moments would stay with him forever.

No. He wasn't supposed to be feeling this much, he

thought. His life wasn't supposed to be changing right here in her arms. But there wasn't a thing he could do to stop it.

Lifting his head, he looked down at her face. Bathed in the dim glow of the bedside lamp, she looked like a goddess just waiting to lead him to paradise.

Words rushed to the tip of his tongue, words that he'd never spoken to any woman, but his throat was too thick to utter a sound. Desperately he tried to swallow the lump away, but emotions continued to build in his chest and surge upward until they were very nearly choking him.

"Bowie? Are you okay?"

He framed her face with his hands, then brought his lips next to hers. "I just want you so much."

As though she understood nothing else needed to be said, she shifted beneath him until her hips were aligned with his. After that there was no holding back. He slid into her slowly, steadily until she surrounded him completely. After that everything became a blur of incredible sensations as blood throbbed against his temples and his body took control of his mind.

Eventually, after he'd managed to catch his breath, he began to move and she followed suit, matching his rhythm as though the two of them had made love to each other for fifty years instead of this being the first time. Perfect. Precious. That was all he could think as he lost himself in the delicious delights of her body.

He wanted this to last forever. For the next several minutes, the thought was like a mantra repeating over and over in his head. And he fought to hold back, to give them one more minute together, and then another. But the need in him kept building higher and stronger until his thrusts reached a frantic pace. Just when he thought his heart would burst right out of his chest, he felt Ava's arms tighten around him and heard her cry out with utter release. Then suddenly, a spectacular vista of shooting stars and night sky suddenly stretched before his eyes. And he was left with no choice but to leap into the gorgeous space and hope he'd eventually land in the safety of Ava's arms.

Long minutes passed before bits of awareness returned to Bowie. Or had it only been a few seconds? His brain was so addled he didn't know. But eventually it dawned on him that the soft warm pillow beneath his cheek was the curve of Ava's breast and the gentle movement against his back was her fingertips sliding up and down the ridges of his spine. Sweat was trickling into his eyes, blurring his vision, but he hardly needed his sight to tell him their bodies were still connected. Her warmth was cradling him with velvety softness, making it even more difficult for him to roll away from her.

"Sorry. I must be squashing you," he murmured while forcing himself to move to one side of her.

She turned toward him and the contented smile on her face thrilled him.

She said, "I was enjoying every ounce of you."

He reached over and threaded his fingers through her long, tangled hair. "A few minutes ago I thought you were beautiful, but now you look…dazzling."

"That's because I feel dazzling." She gingerly touched his arms. "What about you? I hope to heaven I didn't tear any bandages off you."

"I think they're all intact." But after the journey he'd just taken with this woman he couldn't be certain about anything. Except that he was still breathing.

She scooted closer and as her damp skin connected

with his, he was shocked to feel desire stir deep within him again. How could that be when it took every ounce of his strength just to lift his arm?

"And your ankle?"

He chuckled lowly. "Always my little nurse, aren't you?"

She pressed a kiss against the corner of his mouth and the simple contact flooded him with renewed passion and made him want to roll her onto her back and start all over again.

She stroked her fingers across his chest and every spot of skin they touched tingled with anticipation.

"I'm here to heal you. Not hurt you," she murmured.

"You have healed me, Ava. In more ways than you'll ever know."

Doubt flickered in her eyes and then just as quickly it was gone as she smiled and nuzzled her nose against the side of his neck.

"Then I must be a pretty good nurse."

"The best," he whispered against the top of her head.

She said nothing to that and as the room went quiet, he could hear the wind howling. A glance at the window offered him a glimpse of snow splattering against the glass. The winter storm was a paradox to the warmth of her bed, and he hoped the nasty weather wasn't a predictor of their future together.

"It's snowing again," he said.

"I wonder if the party is still going on."

"It'll last a few more hours for sure."

She sighed and snuggled closer. "When we told your father good-night, I thought he gave us that look."

He smiled against her temple. "That look? What kind of *look* are you talking about?"

"The kind that said he knew why we were leaving the party."

His chuckle was riddled with disbelief.

"He couldn't have known. I didn't know it myself."

She eased her head back far enough to look into his eyes. "What made you decide to come back to my room?"

"I was telling myself I needed to be a gentleman. But my empty bedroom was enough to convince me that I'd rather be your lover."

A soft laugh passed her lips and the happy glow in her eyes made Bowie's chest swell with feelings he didn't quite understand.

"A gentleman never keeps a woman waiting," she said. "So you are my gentleman, Bowie Calhoun."

Raw emotion poured through him as he brought his lips back to hers. In a matter of moments, her arms were sliding around his neck and her mouth asking for more. Her needy response quickly hardened his body and when he entered her once again, the thought registered in the back of his mind that this night with Ava was going to change him.

When Ava woke up the next morning, Bowie was no longer by her side. He must have left her room after she'd fallen asleep. Which couldn't have been long ago, since they'd made love until the wee hours of the morning.

What had come over her? She'd gone from telling herself the man was off-limits to climbing into bed with him. Some of that Christmas magic Bowie had been talking about must be affecting her, she thought. Because everything about last night had seemed like a fairy tale. One that she'd never wanted to end.

Sighing, she shoved her tumbled hair away from her

face and turned her head toward a wide span of windows that took up most of one wall of the room. The sheer pink curtains were pulled open, giving her a full view of the snowy sky. It was going to be another cold day, but after spending the night with Bowie she felt warm and incredibly alive.

A knock on the door had her pulling the covers up to her chin. "Come in," she called.

Thinking it had to be Bowie, she was surprised when Tessa entered the room carrying a loaded tray.

"Good morning," she said. "Bowie left orders to bring this up to you at nine o'clock. I was hoping you'd be awake. What with the party going on for so long, you're probably exhausted."

Exhausted wasn't the word for it, Ava thought, as self-conscious heat filled her cheeks. More like exhilarated. She'd forgotten what it was like to have a man give her so much pleasure. Or had she ever really known? Lawrence had been one of those get-to-the-point-quick kind of guys. To have Bowie slowly and thoroughly worshipping every inch of her body was something new and incredible for her.

Hoping none of last night showed on her face, Ava watched the maid carry the tray over to the nightstand and proceed to pour coffee into a china cup balanced on a matching saucer.

Careful to keep the bedcovers over her bare breasts, Ava scooted to a sitting position and accepted the coffee. This would be just a tiny slice of how it must feel to live as a Calhoun, she couldn't help thinking.

"Mmm. This smells delicious. Thank you, Tessa."

"There are warm cinnamon rolls for you, too. Greta just pulled them out of the oven."

"You've gone to far too much trouble for me," Ava told her. "I could've come down to the kitchen."

"You're a guest, Ms. Archer," she said. "Besides, I like you."

Ava sipped her coffee and noticed Tessa looking at the beautiful nightclothes she'd draped over the back of a stuffed armchair. No doubt the maid was curious why Ava wasn't wearing the gown or pajamas. Even worse, she was probably wondering why Ava had chosen to sleep in the nude. Hopefully, Tessa wouldn't connect her lack of clothing to Bowie.

"Uh, is Bowie already up?" Ava dared to ask.

Tessa began to gather Ava's clothes from where Bowie had tossed them to the floor.

"Bowie always rises very early. I guess it's a habit from his military days. Anyway, he's already gone to Carson City. Orin drove him."

Surprised at this news, Ava looked at her. "To town?"

"Yes. He had doctor appointments today. Checkups. Did you forget?"

Now that Ava thought about it, earlier this week Bowie had mentioned the appointments. But with the ER being so swamped for the past several days, the party and then sharing her bed with Bowie, the dates had slipped her mind.

"I had forgotten."

"I believe he expects to be back by midafternoon."

"I have to leave long before then. But that's okay. I'm sure his bandages will be taken care of at the doctor's office."

Tessa said, "Well, I have to go get Mr. Calhoun his morning paper. Before I go, is there anything else I can get for you?"

"No, thanks," she said, but changed her mind as Tessa turned to go. "Uh, there is one thing I'd like to ask you. It's about Bowie. Do you know him very well?"

Tessa paused and the passive expression on her young face had Ava wondering if being a maid in a house full of men had trained the young woman to keep her feelings hidden.

"Ms. Archer, I don't think anyone here knows the real Bowie. He's not one to wear his feelings on the outside. Is there anything wrong?"

"No. I just wondered what you thought about his job. Once he's healthy again, do you think he'll go back to the hotshot crew?"

Tessa thought for a moment. "I believe he will. He likes the excitement. And what he does helps others. You know, save homes and livelihoods. Sometimes those hotshot guys even save lives."

Ava stared thoughtfully into the dark coffee swirling around in her cup. "There's no doubt that it's an admirable job," she agreed.

"Evan once commented that Bowie is like him—he wants to run toward danger rather than away from it. I believe that explains Bowie best."

Ava looked up to see a smile on Tessa's face. "Yes. I think you're right. Thank you, Tessa."

The young woman left the room and Ava did her best to enjoy the coffee and cinnamon rolls. But the nagging reminder of Bowie's job kept getting in the way.

*Why are you thinking about that now? Last night you certainly weren't worried about him being on the hotshot crew. All you could think about was having flaming-hot sex with the man.*

Annoyed at the accusing little voice in her head, Ava

climbed out of bed and marched to the bathroom. She had to be at work in the ER this evening and she wasn't going to get there by lying around, worrying about the future.

But a few minutes later, as the hot shower pelted down on her, she realized that Evan's description of Bowie was very fitting. He would always be a man who wanted to be challenged both mentally and physically. A fact that would often put him in a danger zone. Ava was either going to have to live with that reality, or walk away from him once and for all.

By nine thirty the next morning, Bowie was standing on Ava's front porch, ringing her doorbell. As he waited for her to answer, he noticed that every home on the block had some type of Christmas decorations—lights, nativity scenes, sleighs and reindeer, Santas and elves, and giant candy canes. Each home appeared festive. Except for Ava's. Her little home looked forlorn, a fact that disappointed him.

The door opened and Bowie turned to see a sleepy-eyed Ava stepping onto the small porch with him. She peered suspiciously at the black ranch truck parked in the driveway. "Bowie! What are you doing here? And I don't see a driver!"

"That's because I'm the driver," he said with a happy grin. "I'm finally mobile again. In more ways than one. Look down."

She took one look at his feet and quickly shook her head. "Your cast is gone! Your doctor isn't an orthopedic surgeon, he's a quack!"

Bowie laughed and held up the heavy boot he now wore. "Doc Stillwell is a highly regarded orthopedic surgeon. And I don't think he'd appreciate a nurse calling him a quack." He gestured toward the door. "Uh, do you think we could go inside and get out of this cold?"

His question appeared to jar her back to the present, and she shot him a playful frown. "It's too early in the morning for you to be springing such surprises on me," she said as she opened the door and motioned for him to follow her inside.

"Long night?" he asked.

"I didn't get to bed until after three. One of the nurses was late for the shift change. I had to stay and fill in until she got there."

While she locked the door behind him, he shrugged out of his coat and was about to remove the gray Stetson from his head when she suddenly stopped him.

"Wait," she said. "I want a closer look at you."

"What?"

"In your cowboy hat," she explained. She stepped back to survey him and her eyes sparkled with appreciation. "You look...like a natural."

Her compliment warmed him. "That's because I've had this old thing since I was a teenager. I had Tessa dig it out of the closet for me. I'd forgotten how battered and sweat stained it was. But it's cold outside."

"And it probably feels like a comfortable old glove," she suggested.

"Something like that." He didn't go on to tell her that Rafe had made a big issue of the hat this morning when he'd spotted Bowie leaving the house. He didn't want her thinking, like Rafe, that digging out his old cowboy hat meant his spurs and chaps would be next.

She motioned him toward the kitchen. "Come have coffee and tell me about your checkups."

Bowie was thinking more along the lines of kissing

her until neither of them could breathe, then leading her straight to the bedroom. But he wouldn't. The last thing he wanted was to give Ava the impression he was too young and immature to have anything on his mind but sex.

In the kitchen, Ava gestured for him to take a seat at the little farm table. "I'll get our coffee," she told him.

Once she joined him with two mugs, she sank into a chair kitty-corner to his right. "I'd like to know what you did to get that cast off your foot. Twist the doctor's arm?"

He pulled a playful face at her. "Not hardly. Dad was with me, so I couldn't do much arm twisting. But it wasn't needed. Doc Stillwell said the ankle was healed enough to exchange the cast for a tight-laced work boot. I still have a limp, but he promised that would go away once everything got strengthened again. I have to do exercises for therapy."

"That's great news. And your burns? Was your doctor pleased with their progress?"

He nodded. "Healing nicely. I still have to keep everything covered, though. So that means I'm going to need your nursing skills for a while longer." He slanted her a sly glance. "But now that I persuaded the doctor to let me drive, you won't have to make the long trip out to the ranch. I can drive over here."

She frowned at him. "Absolutely not. Your father hired me to come to the ranch to treat you and that's what I'm going to keep doing. Besides, I'm convinced you have a pair of idiots for doctors. You're in no shape to be driving—or walking."

She rose from the table and walked over to the sink. As she rinsed a cup and small plate beneath the tap, Bowie's gaze drank in the sexy sight she made in her red robe cinched tight at her tiny waist. Her dark hair hung loose against her back and Bowie couldn't stop himself from going over to her and burying his face in the fragrant waves.

"You're too overprotective, Ava," he murmured against her neck. "I can't remain cocooned on the ranch forever. My job, my life, is waiting on me."

Her blue eyes were full of serious shadows as she turned and gazed up at him. "You're right. I think maybe a part of me wants you to stay handicapped just so—well, just so I won't lose you."

Her admission stunned him. "Oh, Ava, darling, you're not going to lose me. Why would you even think that? Even when I'm completely healed I'll still need you in my life. Don't you realize that?"

Lowering her head, she said, "Bowie, our night together was very special for me. But I'm a grown woman, not some naive teenager. I understand that you don't have serious intentions toward me. Honestly, I never expected that from you anyway. But I was talking about losing you in a different way."

With a finger beneath her chin, he drew her face up to his. "You're talking in circles, Ava, and too fast. I'm not following you."

Appearing embarrassed, she covered her face with both hands and quickly stepped around him. "I am going too fast," she said in a strained voice. "I'm sorry."

He turned and with his hands on her shoulders, drew her back against him until he was resting his chin on top of her head and his hands were linked at the front of her waist.

"Don't be sorry, Ava. That's not what I need to hear from you. I want to hear you say you're going to give me—us—a chance. To be together. To figure out exactly what the future might hold for us."

Groaning with anguish, she twisted around in the circle of his arms and buried her face in the middle of his chest. "A future? Oh, Bowie, I don't want to sound like a pathetic old widow, too scared to let her new man walk out the door. That's not how I want to be. But I…" Her words trailed away and she lifted a desperate gaze up to him. "That first day I walked into your room and peeled back those massive bandages, I took one look and knew you'd come close to being killed. To think of you going back to another fire is very scary to me."

He stroked her hair, then cupped her cheek. And as he looked at her it dawned on him that she was the first mature woman he'd had in his life. And he wanted to keep her in it.

The realization stirred something deep within him and though he tried to define it in his mind as sexual chemistry, he knew it was far stronger than that. Yet he wasn't quite willing to call it love. No. Love meant vows and wedding rings, babies and a commitment that would last until God decided to take him from this earth. He wasn't sure he was ready for that. But he was darn sure not ready to let her go, either.

"Your fears come from losing Lawrence," he told her gently.

"Not entirely."

She might think there was more than one cause behind her worries, but that was not the way Bowie saw it. She was still letting her husband's death guide her life. And though he hated that fact, he figured it was a problem that would take a while to fix. But was he man enough to fix it?

"Ava, let's not fret over trouble before it happens. I drove all the way to town to spend time with you. Alone time," he said, lowering his voice to a husky murmur. "I don't want to waste it, do you?"

As he waited for her answer, he gently rubbed the pad of his thumb over her angled cheekbone. After a moment, he was relieved to see a soft light warming the anxious shadows in her eyes. And finally, a slow, inviting smile spread across her lips.

"No," she said gently. "I don't want to waste it."

He kissed her forehead. "You said our night together was special for you. Well, it's all I've been able to think about. You've put a spell on me, honey. And I don't want you to break it."

"A spell, huh?" she whispered. "Perhaps it's some of that Christmas magic you've been talking about."

"Hmm. And it never hurts to start celebrating early."

Her reply was to rise up on her toes and press her lips to his. And that was all it took to make everything fade away. Everything but her.

"If that kiss is my first gift, I can't wait to open the rest of them."

Laughing softly, she took him by the hand and led him to the bedroom.

## *Chapter Nine*

A week later, Christmas was rapidly approaching and Ava had done little about shopping for gifts. Granted, her parents were out of town and had already given her orders not to send gifts, but she still had a few on her list. Most of those people were coworkers. Except for Bowie. What could she possibly buy him—a man who already had everything? And if he didn't already have the things he wanted or needed, he had plenty of money to buy them for himself.

She sighed at the thought, causing Paige to look across the little round table at her. A few minutes earlier the two women had entered the busy shopping mall with its holiday decorations and throngs of shoppers. But before Paige had the chance to push her through the door of the first department store they came to, Ava had lugged her friend to the nearest coffee shop.

"Don't tell me you're tired. We haven't even started yet!" Paige exclaimed.

Shaking her head, Ava picked up her frothy cappuccino. "I'm not tired. I'm trying to figure out what possessed me to come here with you this morning."

"To do your Christmas shopping. That is, we will be shopping once we finish these drinks. Then we're going to hit the stores with a vengeance."

Ava refrained from rolling her eyes. She didn't want to come off as a scrooge, and she truly wanted to get into the holiday spirit. But try as she might, her heart wasn't in it.

"Last week you were complaining about having to go shopping with your mother. I don't know why you were so determined to come today."

Paige shot her an annoyed look. "Because I still have several gifts I need to buy and you haven't even started!" She shook her head. "I might as well have brought my dog with me this morning. He would've been more company."

Ava sipped the warm drink and glanced out at the busy shoppers passing by the coffee shop. Plastic bags dangled from their hands and wrapped boxes were jammed under their arms. A few women were pushing baby carriages, and Ava wondered longingly how it would feel to have children to share her Christmas with, to experience their excitement and joy. She'd probably never know, she thought dismally. Bowie was hardly in the market for a wife and child. And every day she was getting closer to the time when her reproductive organs would shrivel and die. Along with her hopes and dreams of having a family.

Still, Paige deserved better from her today. Ava would have to dig deep and make an effort.

"Sorry, Paige. I'll try to muster up some enthusiasm. I promise."

With a look of concern, Paige reached across the table and touched Ava's hand.

"Ava, what's wrong? You've seemed so happy these past few days and you talked about needing to get out and buy gifts. But now that you're here, you seem miserable."

"I'm just not into the spirit today, Paige. I guess I'm just thinking too much—wondering about things."

"About what? Bowie?"

The mention of his name caused Ava's shoulders to stiffen. A few days ago, Paige had asked her if she'd been seeing Bowie on a personal basis and she'd not been able to lie to her friend. Not that dating Bowie was any kind of secret. Yet sharing the information with Paige had opened Ava's eyes to the whole relationship. She was smack in the middle of a one-sided love affair. One that would eventually end up breaking her heart.

"Partly," she admitted. "He's going to be completely healed from his injuries soon. And after that…"

Paige waited for her to continue, but Ava couldn't find the right words to express the uneasiness she was beginning to feel about the future.

"What? Just because he won't need you as a nurse doesn't mean he'll drop you for another woman. A younger one. Is that what's worrying you?"

Drop her for a younger woman? Funny, but she hadn't worried about that. Maybe because his ardor in the bedroom had seemed to increase instead of wane. "Not exactly. It's his job with the hotshot crew. He doesn't talk about it much, because he knows it troubles me. But I can tell he's excited about going back to work."

"Why should that trouble you? Be glad the man is ambitious enough to want to do such a worthwhile job. With his family's wealth, he could choose a life of leisure. And believe me, there are plenty of guys who'd take advantage of the situation, my ex included."

Ava let out a short laugh. "That's not the Calhoun way. They all work very hard at what they do. And Bowie is no exception. That's why the family is so successful."

"Then what's the problem with him being a firefighter? At least he's not a wimp."

"Paige, the man was nearly killed fighting a wildfire down in Texas! The peak season for fire is over right now, but by midsummer they'll be going strong again and the crew will be sent wherever they're needed. That could be anywhere. Anywhere there's dry brush, mountains and canyons and lightning. Places a firefighter could be trapped or worse. Do you honestly think after losing Lawrence I want to deal with that sort of worry again?"

Her gaze full of compassion, Paige studied her for long moments. "You're in love with him, aren't you? I mean, really in love. The kind of love that never dies."

Paige's observation caused Ava's heart to wince with fatalistic acceptance. For so long, maybe from the moment she'd met Bowie, she'd thought she could simply enjoy his company. His smiles and laughter and easygoing way had woken her long-dead emotions, and she hadn't been able to resist him. But letting herself fall in love with a man nine years her junior? No. She'd never planned on that, but she was very afraid it had already happened.

"Oh, Paige," she muttered helplessly. "I'm such an idiot. Patients are the ones who fall in love with their nurses. Not the other way around. And Bowie is—"

"Quite a hunk," Paige finished for her. "I haven't seen him in the flesh, but I've seen newspaper pictures of him attending some sort of charity function with his family.

I can't imagine what it would be like to have a man like him make love to me. It's no wonder your mind isn't on Christmas shopping."

"There are other things a woman needs to consider about a man—besides sex." And Ava should have considered them long ago, she thought crossly, her cheeks burning.

"Really?" Paige asked, her features wrinkled with comical confusion.

Glad her friend had decided to lighten the moment, Ava pointed to Paige's latte. "Drink up. The mall is jammed with people. If we don't get up and start shopping, all the good stuff is going to be gone."

With an eager smile, Paige picked up her drink. "Now you're talking."


Bowie sat at a long utility table sipping punch from a plastic cup and watching his fellow firefighters laugh over the gag gifts they'd exchanged only minutes earlier. It was good to be back with his group. During the few months he'd worked with the crew, he'd gotten close to all of them. When survival depended on each man watching out for the others, deep friendships tended to develop real fast.

"So how are you making out, Bowie? We've all missed you around here."

Bowie looked up as Rhett Braddock took a seat in the empty folding chair next to his. The dark-haired firefighter was one of the two men who'd pulled him free of the burning tree.

"Hey, Rhett, it's good to see you again. I've been looking for you to show up on the ranch for a visit. But I guess you've been busy."

The other man shook his head. "Sorry, Bowie. I've been planning to come see you. But Dad has been under the weather lately and I've been trying to help him keep things going around the place. He's still hanging on to those cows of his. He won't admit he's not well enough to ranch anymore. But hell, I guess whenever you and I get old, we won't want to give up the things we love, either."

"It's good that he has you to help, Rhett. And good for you that there's not much going right now in the way of wildfires."

"Yeah, the winter break helps," he admitted. "So when are you coming back to work?"

"I'm not a hundred percent yet. My ankle has a ways to go. And the burns aren't totally healed. But the doctors tell me I'll get a green light pretty soon. I'm just thankful I'm finally able to drive again. Being cooped up on the ranch was getting old."

"So you plan on coming back to the crew?"

Surprised by the Rhett's question, Bowie looked at him. "Yes. Why wouldn't I?"

The other man shrugged. "Well, you had a close call down there in the Texas breaks. A thing like that can change a man's way of thinking. None of us guys would blame you if you called it quits."

*I took one look and knew you'd come close to being killed. To think of you going back to another fire is very scary to me.*

Even though Bowie did his best to keep them out, Ava's words suddenly shoved their way into his thoughts. This past week they'd spent as much time together as her job had allowed. And during that time Bowie had slowly begun to see just how much she feared the idea of him returning to firefighting. He didn't want to think it was going to become a problem between them. He continued to hope that, once and for all, she'd push the tragedy of losing Lawrence out of her life. But maybe he was expecting too much from her. Or maybe it was stupid of him to think he could ever mean more to her than her late husband.

"To be honest, Rhett, I don't remember much about those moments before the tree fell. I remember hearing a cracking noise over my head. But the wind was blowing and the smoke was so thick, I could hardly see my hand in front of my face. It was impossible to tell how close the flames had grown. And then, about the time I heard Jamison yelling for us to pull back, the tree came down on me. After that I didn't know anything until I woke up in the hospital. I didn't have time to get scared. Which is a good thing, I suppose. Because it doesn't scare me to think of heading into another fire."

Rhett slanted him a pointed look. "Is your family okay with you returning to the hotshot crew?"

His short laugh held little humor. "No. But they never liked this profession for me in the first place. To hear them tell it, I'm supposed to be on the ranch, watching the cows eat grass and the bulls chase after them."

Rhett let out a mocking grunt. "Sounds like my old man. If I listened to him, I'd be building a fence or driving a hay baler all day long."

Like Bowie, his friend didn't have a mother. From what Rhett had told him, she'd taken off for greener pastures when Rhett had barely been a year old. To Bowie, losing a mother like that was much worse than the tragic accident that had taken his own mother. At least Claudia had been a doting mother to her five sons and daughter and a devoted wife to their father. The memories Bowie had of her were filled with love and a sense of security, and that was a lot more than Rhett would ever have.

From across the room, a coworker suddenly called out, "Hey, Bowie, Rhett, come over here and see if you can take down this dart champion. We're tired of listening to his bragging."

With a good-natured groan, Rhett slowly rose to his feet. "Duty calls."

Glad to focus his thoughts on anything other than family and work, Bowie joined him. "Let's go show these guys who the real champs are around here."

Ava had just finished wrapping the gifts she'd purchased at the mall that morning and was about to get ready to leave for the hospital when Bowie showed up at the front door.

"Well, I thought you must have decided not to get your bandages changed today," she told him as he entered the house. Yesterday he'd told her he'd be driving into town this morning to deal with business and would stop by her place to save her an unnecessary trip to the ranch. But after the time had grown later and later, she'd decided he was going to skip getting his bandages changed altogether.

He shrugged out of his coat and placed it and his hat in the seat of an armchair. "Sorry. I meant to be here an hour ago, but the guys kept talking and it was hard to get away."

"The guys?"

"At the field office. The BLM hotshot crew was holding its annual Christmas party," he explained.

In spite of the room being cozy and warm, Ava felt chilled to the bone. Yet she did her best to hide her reaction from Bowie. A few days ago, she'd told him she didn't want to come off as some sort of harried widow, and she'd meant that. Besides, Bowie didn't belong to her. She had no right to cling to him or tell him what he should do with his life.

"Oh. So you've been celebrating with your coworkers. That's nice."

"It was nice to be with all the guys again," he agreed.

She shut the door and started to step around him, but he quickly snatched her wrist and pulled her into the circle of his arms. As he anchored his hands at the sides of her waist, he said, "But it's not nearly as nice as this."

He bent his head and kissed her, but Ava could only give him a lukewarm response, one that had him cocking a questioning brow at her.

"What's wrong?"

She avoided his gaze by concentrating on his denim shirt. "Nothing. I just don't have much time before I have to leave for work."

"Sorry," he repeated. "Time got away from me."

"It has a way of doing that when you're having fun."

He let out a long breath. "Are you angry at me for going to the party instead of coming here to see you?"

She groaned. "No. Of course not. I'm not that childish, Bowie. Besides, I've been out shopping for most of the day."

"Oh, Christmas shopping?"

The eagerness in his voice was like that of an excited little boy who couldn't wait for Santa to arrive. The sound was contagious, and she looked up at him and smiled. "That's right. I figured if I didn't get you something you'd call me Ms. Scrooge."

"Never." His features turned serious as he drew her closer. "You're really not mad at me?"

"No. But later I think we need to talk."

Clearly annoyed by her announcement, he shoved out a heavy breath. "Oh, hell. I really don't want to hear this right now, Ava."

His reaction stung. Particularly since she'd not asked him for any kind of promises. "What do you mean? You don't like hearing that I need to talk to you? Well, pardon me for the inconvenience."

"Ava, any time a man hears 'we need to talk,' he knows things between him and his woman are going south."

Her brows shot straight up. "Your woman? Really, Bowie? That's news to me."

He looked stunned, but Ava didn't care. Days had gone by since she'd given herself to this man, and she was coming to the bleak reality that nothing between them was going to change. The fire of passion was going to burn out and she was going to be left with nothing but a broken heart.

"Ava, where is all this coming from? What do you want from me? Yesterday when I left, you kissed me like you never wanted to let me go. I don't understand."

Closing her eyes, she turned away and tried to swallow the foolish tears collecting in her throat. She wasn't making sense. And she didn't know why all of this had suddenly burst out of her. But when he'd shown up late and she'd learned he'd been with the hotshot crew, something inside her had snapped.

"Maybe that's what happens when your woman is nine years older than you," she said thickly.

"That doesn't even deserve a response. So what is this?

You've decided to have a pity party for yourself? Don't you think it would be better to have a Christmas party?"

Anger snapped her teeth together and then just as quickly it drained away. "I'm sorry, Bowie. I sound like a shrew. And you don't deserve that."

She moved toward the doorway leading out of the living room, and Bowie followed close on her heels. "Ava, it's clear you're unhappy with me. Tell me why. Please."

So now he wanted to talk? She wanted to scream. Instead, she reminded herself that this whole situation was her fault, not his. "Bowie, I don't have time for this. And it doesn't matter anyway. All of this is my problem. Not yours."

She entered the bedroom where she'd already laid out her uniform across the bed. Bowie trailed after her and stood to one side while she began to change.

"I didn't know you had a problem," he said. "Since the night of the party we've been together every day. I thought things were going good for us."

"I did, too. Until today."

She pulled a white slip over her head then smoothed it down over her hips. All the while she could feel Bowie's eyes watching her. Not as a man enjoying the view of a woman's curves, but like a man who was trying to figure out who this Ava was and why she'd suddenly made an appearance.

"I went shopping. I saw people. I saw—"

She'd seen mothers and fathers with babies and children. She'd seen families preparing for the holiday together. How could she explain the emptiness that had come over her? For a long time she'd been afraid to even think about trying to be a wife again or, God willing, a mother. But Bowie had come along and opened her eyes.

Making love to him had made her see she was wasting precious time. He wasn't a family man and she'd be wrong to try to change him into one.

"I saw a lot of things about myself, Bowie. I guess that's what I'm trying to say."

She sat down on a dressing bench at the foot of the bed and began to pull on her panty hose. Bowie came to stand in front of her. "Do you want to quit seeing me? Is that what you're telling me?"

Just hearing him ask the question was like a lance right between her breasts. And though her mind was telling her to make a quick break and get it over with, her heart was begging her to wait, to find a way they could fit their lives together.

With her stockings in place, she rose to her feet, and as she dared to meet his gaze, tears filled her eyes.

"No. I don't want us to end things. But—"

He didn't allow her to finish. Instead he snatched her into his arms and roughly covered her mouth with his. This time, as he began to kiss her, Ava couldn't hold back. Her lips clung hungrily to his, telling him in no uncertain terms how much she still wanted him.

Eventually the need for air forced the kiss to end, and he pressed his cheek against hers. "Ava, sweet darling, we've only been together a short time. We're still getting to know one another. I don't know exactly what you want from me. But I know what I want—and that's you, right here in my arms. Are you sure you don't have a few minutes before you need to leave?"

The sound of his husky voice and the warmth of his breath against her cheek was Ava's undoing. She slipped her arms around his neck. "Fifteen minutes, tops," she whispered.

"Perfect," he replied and with a growl of pleasure he guided her backward until she was lying flat on her back in the middle of the bed.

A week later, when Ava walked into the nurses' locker room to put her things away before the start of the shift, Paige was already there. The moment she spotted Ava, her mouth flew open.

"What are you doing here? It's Christmas Eve. I thought you were off this evening."

She certainly needed the time off, Ava thought wearily. The past six days had passed in a wild blur. Every night, the ER had been incredibly busy. Between working and spending every spare minute she could with Bowie, she'd hardly slept, much less had time to think. But she was going to have to make herself do some serious thinking, and quick. The man was taking her on a romantic ride with an unknown destination. She needed to decide whether she was going to follow him all the way to a dead end or jump off before her heart was completely shattered.

Trying not to dwell on her situation with Bowie, she said, "Whoever put up the shift roster wasn't aware that I had agreed to swap days with Judith."

"But why did you promise to work in her place? Aren't you going to the Silver Horn to be with Bowie?"

"I promised Judith long before Bowie and I—well, started seeing each other. Besides, tonight's a family affair on the Silver Horn and I'm not family. So I invited him to my place for Christmas dinner tomorrow."

Paige frowned as she whipped her auburn hair into a ballerina bun and secured it with a giant clip. "So what if you're not family now? You might be a Calhoun in the future," she pointed out.

Ava opened her locker and shoved her shoulder bag inside. "That's not likely to happen."

Paige pulled a white cardigan over her black scrubs. As she buttoned it, she eyed Ava curiously.

"Do you want it to happen?" she asked.

Ava sighed. This past week Bowie couldn't have been more attentive or caring, yet a melancholy cloud had hovered over her in spite of the pleasurable hours she'd spent with him. And why? Because the deepest part of her heart had started to hope he'd say something about love and their future. And so far he'd said nothing about either one. Maybe she was expecting too much too soon from him. Or maybe she'd been deceiving herself all along into believing she might actually become that important to him.

"For the past several days I've been asking myself that question over and over."

"And?"

Ava shut the locker and twisted the combination lock. "It's pointless, Paige. Even if Bowie loved me, which he doesn't, he's not interested in a wife or kids."

"How do you know that for sure? Have you talked to him about it? Have you told him you love him?"

Ava glanced over at a pair of nurses on the other side of the small room. At the moment, the older women both appeared to be tending to their own business rather than listening to hers.

Lowering her voice a notch, she said, "Bowie told me from the very beginning he wasn't in the market for a family. Like a fool, I fell in love with him anyway. And no. I haven't told him how I feel about him. How do you tell a guy something he doesn't want to hear?"

"Then what exactly are you doing with the man, Ava?" As soon as the question was out of Paige's mouth, she slapped her forehead. "Sorry. Forget I asked that question. Let's just get to work."

Because it was Christmas Eve, a few of the nurses had brought candy and Helen had baked a huge Italian cream cake to share with her coworkers during breaks. Ava was glad to see everyone in the spirit of the holiday, even though she could hardly muster any appetite for the treats.

While her fellow nurses celebrated, she continued to think about Bowie and the question Paige had thrown at her. Exactly what was she doing with the man? Besides going to bed with him?

Last week, when Ava had tried to tell him her concerns about their relationship, he'd put her off. Instead of listening to her worries, he'd thought the solution had been to take her to bed. Making love to Bowie was always incredible, but he needed to understand there was a world outside the bedroom. On the other hand, she needed to remember she'd had her eyes wide open when she'd walked into an affair with him. She couldn't expect him to change just for her.

As the evening shift in the ER wore on, the typical holiday patients began to trickle through the doors. Partygoers with a bit too much alcohol in their systems were treated for cuts, gashes and sprains from falling. And a few children suffering stomachaches from consuming too much rich food needed attention. However, on this Christmas Eve Ava hadn't been expecting a gunshot victim. Especially when it turned out to be the detective who worked as Evan Calhoun's partner.

When Vincent Parcell arrived in the ER, he was bleeding profusely from the shoulder and suffering internal bleeding from another gunshot to the abdomen. Dr. Sherman stabilized him as best he could, then ordered him to emergency surgery.

Two male nurses were hurriedly pushing the patient toward the elevator when another patient with cardiac arrest was wheeled into the treatment area. As Dr. Sherman rushed to his side, Paige turned to Ava.

"I think Detective Calhoun is still in the waiting room," she said. "Dr. Sherman doesn't have time to give him an update on his partner. It might be easier coming from someone he knows."

"All right," Ava told her. "I'll give him what information we have."

Paige hurried away to assist Dr. Sherman and Ava made her way to the waiting room to find Detective Calhoun.

She'd only met Evan a few times, the last time being two weeks ago at the Silver Horn Christmas party. As far as she could tell he didn't show up on the ranch that frequently, but Bowie spoke of his older brother often, and she knew he admired him greatly.

Detective Calhoun was standing next to the plate glass wall that overlooked a small courtyard on the hospital grounds. Although the night sky was clear, snow from the previous days was still piled against a tall concrete fountain and the bare bushes and benches. It was a dismal view for a man who'd just been in a gunfight, she thought.

"Mr. Calhoun?"

He whirled around and Ava was immediately struck

by how much he resembled Bowie. Although Evan's hair was much darker, he had those green Calhoun eyes and a faint set of dimples in his cheeks.

Two quick strides had the detective standing in front of Ava, and he promptly reached out to shake her hand. "Ms. Archer, I'm glad to see you. Can you tell me anything about Vince?"

"Dr. Sherman had to attend to another critical patient, so I'll tell you what I know. Mr. Parcell has wounds to the shoulder and the abdomen. Dr. Sherman managed to slow the blood loss in the shoulder wound, but the internal bleeding has to be dealt with in surgery. He's already on his way there."

Evan blew out long breath and Ava could see he was terribly distressed.

"How was he? I mean, is he critical? Will he make it?"

Trying to walk a fine line between caution and optimism, she said, "Mr. Parcell has lost a lot of blood, but the doctors are already starting to deal with that problem. His vitals are weak, but stable, especially considering his wounds. Once his internal injuries are repaired, he should make it. Barring anything unexpected, that is."

He lifted a brown cowboy hat from his head and wiped a shaky hand through his hair. "I see. Well, how long do you think he'll be in surgery?"

"That depends on the extent of his injuries. But I expect it will be a while."

He plopped the hat back on his head and Ava noticed he had blood smeared on one sleeve and the front of the sheriff's department jacket he was wearing.

"Are you okay, Mr. Calhoun?" she asked anxiously. "Do you need a doctor, too?"

Shaking his head, he glanced down at himself. "This

blood is all Vince's. After he was hit, we were trying to make it back to the vehicle, but he collapsed in my arms."

"I'm so sorry. But your partner is in the best of care now. Let's pray and think positive."

"Believe me, I've already been doing a lot of praying, Ms. Archer."

She pointed toward a wide corridor. "Right down there is a set of elevators. Ride one up to the fourth floor and you'll find a waiting area outside the operating rooms. Is any of your family coming to be with you? I can contact Bowie. I know he'd be glad to give you some company."

"Thanks, but the sheriff and two deputies are already on their way here. Some Christmas Eve, huh?"

She gave him an encouraging smile. "Try not to worry."

Already striding toward the elevators, he looked back over his shoulder. "Thanks. I'll remind Bowie you're a keeper."

As Bowie drove from the Silver Horn to Ava's house, he spoke to Evan and learned that Vince was holding his own after yesterday's surgery and the doctors expected him to pull through. Bowie was relieved, especially for his brother's sake. Evan and Vince had worked closely together for several years. They were like brothers.

In spite of the good news, Bowie wasn't feeling the high spirits he normally experienced on Christmas Day. Perhaps that was due to his family being separated this year. Other than Bowie, the only ones to gather around the tree this morning to open gifts had been Grandfather Bart, Clancy and his wife, Olivia, and their baby son, Shane.

His father, along with Rafe and his whole family, had

driven up to Alturas, California, to visit Finn, Mariah and baby Harry. Evan was clearly tied up with the overnight shooting incident and it appeared unlikely he'd be able to bring his family to the Silver Horn for any kind of celebration.

But if Bowie wanted to be totally honest with himself, none of that was the root cause of his dejected mood. Something was wrong with Ava. Even though she'd made love to him and even though she was having him over for Christmas dinner, he sensed that she was about to rip his world apart. And he didn't know what to do about it.

Yet minutes later, when Ava met him at the door and ushered him inside, he left most of his worries on the porch. She was wearing a red dress that stopped just below her knees and draped every curve just right. A pair of black high heels were on her feet, while rhinestones glittered on her earlobes and around her neck. Her long dark hair was pinned up in a way that left little tendrils dangling against the back of her neck and around her face.

"Merry Christmas, Ava. You look incredible," he told her as he kissed her cheek.

She gave him a warm smile. "Merry Christmas to you, too. You look pretty good yourself."

He placed the two gifts he was carrying on the coffee table. "So tell me, did Santa come by last night?"

She feigned a pouting look. "When I got home from work, I didn't find a thing. Someone must have told him I've been naughty."

He gave her a wicked smile. "You're in luck. I think naughty girls should get gifts, too."

She laughed softly and Bowie was relieved to see she was in a festive mood. Maybe the uneasiness he'd been feeling these past couple of days was really nothing. At least, he was going to do his best to believe that.

"Dinner is almost ready," she told him. "Do you want to eat before we open our gifts?"

He glanced at the gifts on the coffee table, then back to her. "Let's eat first. When you open your gifts I don't want you to be distracted."

She slanted him a coy look. "Guess you'll have to leave the room, then."

Groaning with pleasure, he gathered her into his arms and kissed her Christmas-red lips. She tasted like coffee and whipped cream and something undefinable— like his future.

The notion shook him, yet he was determined not to shy away from his thoughts. For the past few days, he'd been dreaming, planning and trying to figure out where Ava belonged in his future. Now that he'd decided exactly what she meant to him, he wasn't at all sure how she was going to react if and when he told her.

"You are a naughty girl," he said with a chuckle, then clasped his hand around hers. "Come on. I'm dying to see what we're going to eat."

"Don't get too excited. I didn't have enough time to cook much. I have to confess that some of it I bought already prepared. But everything tastes good."

She led him to the kitchen and as Bowie helped her put the meal onto the table, he said, "I talked to Evan briefly a few minutes ago. He says Vince's condition is stable and slightly improved. He sounded relieved, but hardly in the holiday spirit. I think he blames himself for Vince getting shot."

"Sometimes things like that can't be helped."

Like her late husband being mortally wounded, Bowie

thought grimly. Vince's trauma was probably a sad reminder to her, especially here at the holiday. But she'd had thirteen years to come to terms with her husband's loss and the dangers men faced. Surely she was strong enough to deal with them now. After all, she worked in the ER, where trauma was an everyday experience.

"By the way, thanks for texting last night to let me know about Evan and Vince. I wanted to join him at the hospital, but he was tied up with the sheriff and the ongoing investigation of the shooting. I would've only been in the way."

"I felt so awful for him," she said as she placed a bowl of fruit salad on the table. "Will your brother have time today to spend with his wife and baby?"

"He thinks he'll get off work tonight. Noelle and baby Joanna went over to spend some of the day with Sassy and Jett and their kids. The two ranching women are close, so Noelle will have good company until Evan gets home."

She moved around the table until she was close enough to slip her arms around his waist. "And I have good company, too." She tilted her head back and smiled wistfully up at him. "My Christmas wouldn't mean much without you, Bowie."

"You're the best Christmas gift I could ever have." He kissed her, then gestured toward the table. "Let's eat before I'm the one who gets distracted."

With everything served, Ava lit two tall green candles positioned in the center of the table and they took their seats. Bowie said a quick prayer over the food and they began to enjoy the baked ham, candied yams and green bean casserole, along with several other rich dishes.

Bowie had very nearly finished the food on his plate

and was trying to decide if he had room for a piece of pecan pie when her cell phone rang.

"Excuse me, Bowie. I'd better make sure that's not the hospital calling. I'm not supposed to go in until tonight, but things happen." She rose from the table and went over to the cabinet to answer her phone.

Bowie's spirits sank. It was bad enough that she had to work the ER tonight. He didn't want to have to give up this afternoon with her.

And then he heard her say, "No, Mom. We're eating now. That's right. I'm not alone."

Ava had never talked much to Bowie about her parents, and he'd simply assumed she wasn't that close to either one of them. But today was Christmas, so it was probably no surprise her mother had called.

After another long pause Ava asked, "Oh, what is it? You're coming home sooner than you thought?"

She went silent and Bowie noticed her face taking on a pale hue. Apparently, her mother had told her something upsetting.

"Are you kidding? Okay, put him on." Seconds later, she said in a choked voice, "Hi, Daddy. Yes, I'm stunned. It's okay. Yes, merry Christmas. I love you. See you soon."

She ended the call, then looked at Bowie and promptly burst into tears.

## Chapter Ten

Instantly Bowie was on his feet. "Ava, what's wrong? What's happened?" he asked anxiously.

Taking her by the shoulders, he pulled her into the shelter of his arms. She sniffed back tears and when she finally looked up at him, Bowie could see her blue eyes were clouded with confusion.

"That was my parents. They called to wish me a merry Christmas and to tell me they're getting married again. Married! I don't know. It's all such a shock."

Relieved that there wasn't an emergency, he said in a bemused voice, "I'd think that would be happy news."

She frowned. "That's because you don't know the situation. They argued continually while they were married."

"Not always," Bowie pointed out. "They had you."

She rolled her eyes at him. "You would think in those terms."

He gently rubbed his forefinger beneath her chin. "Could be that things have changed with them. People are capable of changes, if they want to make them badly enough."

Sighing, she turned her back to him and bent her head. "A part of me is happy, Bowie. But it didn't work with my parents before. What if it doesn't work now? What if—"

"Ava," he interrupted, "listen to yourself. Why are you worrying about things going wrong instead of being happy that your parents are brave enough to try again?"

She turned back to him and her lips were parted with surprise, as though she hadn't realized until this moment how she sounded.

"I don't know why I feel this way, Bowie."

"Well, I think I do," he said flatly. "You've been unhappy for so long you believe wrong is the only way things can go."

She frowned at him. "Look, we're not talking about your parents here, Bowie. It's easy for you to take a casual view of the situation."

He wanted to shake her. Instead, he said, "No. We're not talking about my parents. Because my mother is dead. My parents weren't given a second chance to live the rest of their lives together."

A sheepish expression stole over her features. "I'm sorry, Bowie. I—I don't understand what's wrong with me. Or why I'm crying or worrying. For years now I've wanted my parents to get married again. Now that they are, the only thing I can think about is the two of them breaking each other's hearts all over again."

He studied her for long moments, then took her by the hand to lead her out of the kitchen. "Come on," he urged. "You need something else to think about. Let's go open our gifts."

When they reached the small living room, Ava collected a rather large gift from the coat closet and set it alongside the ones he'd placed on the coffee table. After they sat close together on the couch, Bowie reached for a thin square box wrapped in bright red-and-gold paper and offered it to her.

"Open this one first," he said.

She handed him his one and only gift and together they began removing ribbons and tearing paper.

Ava was the first to get hers open, and she gasped with pleasure when she spotted a cream-colored sweater made of incredibly soft cashmere.

"Oh, this is so lovely, Bowie. And the color will go with everything!"

"I'm not up on women's fashion, but I was sure it would look good on you," he said with an appreciative grin.

She held up the sweater for a better look, while Bowie tore away the last of the paper on his own gift. When he finally lifted the lid on the heavy box, he found a pair of snub-toed cowboy boots in dark burgundy leather. The tall shafts were decorated with intricate inlays of red and turquoise in the shape of a thunderbird.

"These are incredible!" Amazed, he looked at her. "Ava, these were obviously very expensive. You shouldn't have spent this much!"

Smiling wanly, she said, "The leather isn't anything exotic, but the boots reminded me of you. The thunderbird is handsome and proud and free—like you."

He leaned over and placed a tender kiss on her lips.

"Thank you, Ava. As soon as my ankle gets completely well, this will be the first pair of boots I pull on."

With the boot box still on his lap, he picked up the remaining gift on the coffee table and handed it to her. "Now it's your turn again," he said gently. "Merry Christmas, darling."

The sudden tenderness in Bowie's voice should have warned Ava that something special was inside the long rectangular box, but she wasn't prepared to find a white satin pouch with a ring inside. A large tear-shaped ruby was surrounded by two rows of smaller diamonds that glittered beneath the light. It was stunning and nothing like anything she'd ever dreamed of owning.

Totally awed, she whispered, "Bowie, this is— You certainly know how to surprise a woman."

"Do you like it?"

Her heart beating fast, she looked up at him. "It's so, so lovely. But it's far too expensive. I—"

Before she could go on, he plucked the ring from its blanket of satin, then reached for her hand.

"Let's see if it fits. I guessed at the size, so I might have to get the jeweler to resize it for you."

He started to push the ring onto her finger when it suddenly dawned on Ava that he was holding her left hand.

"Bowie, you have the wrong hand." She thrust her right hand toward him. "This finger will most likely be a different size."

He shook his head. "I know what I'm doing. An engagement ring goes on your left hand."

Ava gasped. "Engagement? Bowie, what are you talking about?"

Smiling smugly, he pushed the beautiful ring onto her

finger. "I realize this isn't what you'd call a conventional engagement ring, but I wanted you to have something different and special. Because you are different and special."

Amazingly, the ring was a perfect fit, yet as Ava stared at the beautiful stones, she was bombarded with conflicting emotions. Joy, fear, confusion and elation were spinning through her.

"Am I supposed to assume that this ring means you love me?"

He drew her hand to his lips and kissed the back of her fingers. "I don't want you to assume anything, Ava. I'm telling you—I love you. I want you to be my wife."

Just hearing him say those three little words caused her heart to swell with joy. But the practical part of her refused to believe he could suddenly be in love with her, much less be her husband.

Lifting her gaze back to his, she stared at him in disbelief. "Bowie, I don't know what to say. This is so sudden. And you—"

Drawing on both her hands, he pulled her closer. "I realize it seems sudden to you. But not to me. I've been thinking about this from the first day I met you."

Even more skeptical now, she shook her head. "Bowie, the first day you met me, the only thing on your mind was sex."

"Since when did nurses become mind readers?"

She groaned. "Oh, Bowie, even a blind woman could've figured you out that day. And the day after. And—"

"Okay," he relented. "Maybe it's taken me a while to figure out my feelings. But that doesn't make them any less real."

She wanted so very much to believe him. In a short time, he'd become everything to her. Yet that didn't mean he was the right man for her. It didn't mean that months from now, she'd be happy.

"You aren't ready for this, Bowie," she said flatly. "Not love. Not marriage. And you're certainly not ready for me."

Frustration twisted his features. "I suppose you're going to use the age argument on me. Well, that won't fly, Ava. I might be younger than you, but I'm not stupid. I know my own mind."

Her doubtful gaze searched his rugged features. "Saying you love me, giving me a ring—that's the easy part. And me saying yes to you—that would be the easiest thing I've ever done in my life. But what would happen afterward? You're going to be well soon. And it's obvious to me that you plan on going back to the hotshot crew."

He let out a heavy breath. "That's my job, Ava. It's what I trained for. Maybe in your eyes that doesn't mean as much as the training you went through to become a nurse, but it's important to me."

Love for this man was pouring from her heart, making her whole body ache to be in his arms, to surrender to everything he wanted.

Leaning closer, she gently cupped his left cheek in her palm. "Bowie, I'm not trying to demean your work. I actually admire the good you do and the courage it takes to face all that danger. It's just not something I can live with."

The look in his eyes was almost accusing. "There's one thing I've not heard from you in all of this, Ava. You haven't bothered to mention how you feel about me. Does that count for anything?"

Tears were suddenly clawing the back of her eyes. But rather than try to blink them away, she simply closed her eyes and swallowed hard. "I love you, Bowie. I've known that ever since the night of the party. But that doesn't fix anything."

"Well, that's something, at least." He left the couch and walked over to the picture window. As he stood, legs apart, staring at her front lawn, he said, "I'm beginning to understand why your yard is bare of Christmas decorations. Why there's no tree or tinsel or mistletoe inside. It's because you don't want to believe. You don't want to let yourself celebrate love and life."

He might as well have stabbed her in the chest, but she refused to let a tear fall. He didn't know what it was like to have a spouse ripped away, to have all his dreams and plans taken away in the blink of an eye. He'd never had to live in a house by himself. He couldn't know the endless silence, the loneliness, the longing to be touched and loved and protected.

"Think what you will, Bowie, because there's no way I can make you understand how I really feel." Compelled to be near him, she left the couch and walked over to where he stood. When he turned toward her, she instinctively reached for his hand and curled her fingers tightly around his. "All I can say is that I lost one husband to a dangerous job. I can't live with the fear of going through that again. I could ask you to give up your job. But that would be wrong of me. And even if you were willing to find a different profession, you wouldn't be happy, and then you'd end up blaming me for your misery. Don't you see, Bowie? We just can't fit things together."

His shook his head as though he couldn't believe what he was hearing. "You're right, Ava, I don't understand. If this is the way you feel—if you knew this all along—why did you let things go so far with us? Why the hell did you even go to bed with me in the first place?"

Astonished that he could even ask such a thing, she dropped his hand and put a few steps between them. After taking several breaths to calm herself, she realized the effort was useless.

"Are you kidding me?" she asked, unable to keep the emotion from her voice. "Are you honestly going to try to make me believe you had marriage on your mind that first night we had sex? I might have seemed pretty damn easy to you, but I'm not totally stupid, Bowie."

"All right," he snapped. "Maybe I didn't know then that things were going to turn serious. And you didn't, either. But later you should've told me there wasn't any chance for us to have a future together. Instead, you made love to me like—like you really meant it!"

He was angry, but then so was she. Angry because he wasn't trying in the least to see her side of things. And angry, too, because she couldn't see any way the problem standing between them could ever be solved.

Turning her back to him, she muttered in a low, painful voice, "You're right. And yesterday when you were here, I tried. But you didn't want to hear it."

Suddenly he was standing behind her, his hands wrapped over her shoulders, and it was all Ava could do to keep from turning and flinging herself into his arms and telling him she'd marry him in a heartbeat.

"Ava, what do you want me to do? Listen to my family and be a cowboy the rest of my life?"

She twisted around to face him and her heart winced as she spotted the anguish clouding his eyes.

"Would that be so bad, Bowie? To work with your

brothers and father? The Silver Horn is a very special place."

His lips took on a rueful slant. "Now it's you who doesn't understand," he said. "I don't want to be just a token hand. No matter what job I'm doing, I want my work to make a difference—to mean something. Rafe and Dad are cowboys at heart. That makes them good at what they do. I'm not like them."

Her nostrils flared as she struggled to keep a grip on her crumbling emotions. "You talk about me being afraid, Bowie. Well, I think it's about time you go home and take a look in the mirror. You've been running from yourself ever since you became old enough to call yourself a man."

At her words, his eyes widened. "Running? You don't know what you're talking about. I went into the Marines. You think that didn't take guts?"

"Of course it did. But it would've taken more guts to stay on the Silver Horn and prove to your father and your grandfather that you are just as worthy of a position on the ranch as your brothers."

Instead of being outraged by her accusation, he went silent and pale, and though it hurt Ava to know she'd struck a deep nerve in him, she'd felt compelled to open his eyes to the truth.

Tension hung in the air as she waited for him to speak. When he did, his voice was as flat and empty as her bare front yard.

"That's what you think?" he asked.

"That's what I know."

"Then I'm wasting my time here." He turned away from her and retrieved his hat and coat. After jerking them on, he picked up the boot box and shoved it beneath one arm. "Thanks for the boots, Ava. Too bad I can't fill them for you."

Her heart splintering into a million painful pieces, she walked over to him and pulled the ring from her finger. "Here. I guess you'd better take this."

He took the ring from her and placed it in her palm. As he folded her hand tightly over it, he said in a strained voice, "The ring is a Christmas gift. Wear it as one. And maybe one of these days you'll look at it and wonder why you were too scared to become my wife."

Dry-eyed, she watched him walk out the door and shut it behind him. But once she heard his truck fire up and drive away, she couldn't stop the acid tears of regret from sliding down her face.

Ten days later, the hubbub of the holidays was over and the Silver Horn was back to its normal routine. In a few weeks, new calves would begin to drop and the mares would keep the foaling barn busy around the clock. At this time of the year anything could happen with the weather, and the ranch hands could either be digging baby calves out of the snow or watching them play in the warm sun.

As for Bowie, he expected his doctors to give him a medical release to return to work in the next few days. He'd healed more quickly than expected and the realization of getting back to his normal routine should be filling him with happy anticipation. Instead, he was miserable.

"Bowie, I'm not sure about this one piece of tape," his father said as he fumbled with the bandage. "It might not hold. It sure doesn't want to stick to your skin."

Bowie stared at the floor in front of him and tried to hold on to his patience. For the past five minutes, Orin had been struggling to tape the light bandage onto Bowie's shoulder. After he'd walked out of Ava's house on Christmas Day, she'd called Orin and told him he'd have to find a different nurse to care for Bowie. Understanding his son wasn't in any mood to deal with a new nurse, his father had kindly offered to take on the chore.

"Don't worry about it, Dad. My burns are healed now. The bandages are just to protect the new skin."

"That's right. But the new skin is as thin as onion paper. We got to make sure it's protected." He stepped back and handed Bowie his shirt. "There. I think you're good to go."

"Thanks, Dad." Bowie slipped on his shirt and while he dealt with the buttons, he noticed his father standing to one side waiting. "You want to talk with me or something?"

Orin smiled. "Or something. I want you to go down to the horse barn with me. The new stallion has arrived. I'd like to have your opinion on him."

For the past ten days, both Orin and Rafe had found every excuse to get Bowie out and about on the ranch. At first he'd thought their efforts stemmed from his breakup with Ava. He hadn't done a very good job of hiding his misery, and Bowie figured his family believed keeping him occupied would help lift his spirits. But now he was beginning to see they were making a full-fledged effort to get him involved in ranching again.

*It would've taken more guts to stay on the Silver Horn and prove to your father and grandfather that you are just as worthy of a position on the ranch as your brothers.*

Ava's words continued to haunt him. Because the more he thought about them, the more he wondered if she'd been right. Had he run off to the Marines all those years ago because he'd not wanted to compete against his brothers for a position on the ranch? Was that why he'd gone straight into firefighting as soon as he'd returned home? Because he was still afraid to try to find his rightful place on the Silver Horn?

He didn't know what to think anymore. Not about himself or her. He only knew that life without Ava was pure hell.

"I'll go, but I'm not sure my opinion will be worth anything."

Bowie rose to his feet and walked over to the closet to collect his coat. Orin stood at the bedroom door, watching him with a keen eye.

"You're walking much smoother now. How does the ankle feel, now that you've been out of that cast for a while?"

"Still a little stiff. But it's great to be out of the cast and to be able throw that damned crutch away."

"Well, it's great to see you back on your feet, son." He slung his arm affectionately around Bowie's shoulder. "That first day I saw you in the hospital down in Amarillo—I'll be honest, it scared the hell out of me. You weren't even coherent."

"I had a concussion and they'd given me something for the pain," Bowie explained in an effort to downplay the severity of his injuries.

"No matter. Other than losing your little two-year-old sister, Darci, to a heart defect, I'd never seen any of my children hurt. Not badly. I won't lie, Bowie, it was hard on me."

Since Bowie had returned to the ranch to recuperate, his father hadn't said much about the accident or Bowie's injuries. It surprised him that he was talking about it this morning.

"I'm sorry I put you through the worry, Dad. It was a freak thing. I mean, the Texas Panhandle is not a place known for trees. You can drive for miles and not see even one. When I tell folks where I was and that a tree fell on me, they think I'm crazy."

Orin said, "I've been in that area they call the breaks. There are plenty of trees in some of those canyons. The way your captain explained it, the deepness of the arroyo was causing a downdraft in the wind. It made the fire explode." He patted Bowie's good shoulder, then opened the door and ushered him through it. "That's enough about that stuff, though. Let's go have a look at the stallion."

As he and his father walked over to the horse barn, Bowie fully expected Orin to use the moment to go into a speech about needing and wanting him to remain on the ranch. But surprisingly his father didn't bring up the subject, and by the time they entered the barn, Bowie decided he could relax and let his guard down.

Maybe his father was like Ava. He'd given up on the notion of Bowie becoming a cowboy again, he thought. Then he wondered why that notion left him feeling even worse.

Ava sat in her mother's kitchen, watching the woman fill a cardboard box with her finest china. She could hear her father out in the living room, taking down photos and paintings from the walls.

"So do you have anyone to keep an eye on this place after you leave?" Ava asked her mother.

The trim blonde continued to carefully wrap a dinner plate in newspaper. "Yes. I have a friend who's going to stop by every day to make sure nothing is amiss. And the real estate agent assures me it will be a quick sell."

Ava didn't know what to think or how to feel. Her parents had already gotten married on New Year's Day, and by the end of the week Velda and Stu would be making their home down in San Diego, where her father still worked at an investment firm.

"Are you sure you really want to get rid of this place?" Ava questioned her mother. "I've always thought it was so pretty with the pool and the willows and the big front lawn."

"It is pretty and I've enjoyed living here. But it's no comparison to being with your father."

Concern marking her brow, Ava went to her mother's side. Then lowering her voice so that her father wouldn't hear, she said, "Mom, it hasn't been that long ago that you were saying if you two were together too much, you'd be fighting. Has something changed? What makes you think this time will be any different?"

The look her mother turned on her was pure disappointment. "Ava, I've prayed for years that you'd lose this pessimistic attitude of yours. But you keep hanging on to it like a kid with a safety blanket. You can't ever look on the hopeful side of things, can you?"

Dear Lord, her mother was sounding just like Bowie. He'd also accused her of being all gloom and doom. Was that really the way people saw her? It was a sickening thought.

"You're evading the question, Mom."

Heaving out an annoyed breath, Velda went back to wrapping the dinner plates. "Okay. There's nothing different going on with your father and me, except that we love each other enough to want to try again. You see, we've learned that we're miserable without each other. And we're determined to keep things right this time around."

"I see. Well, I wish—" Ava broke off abruptly and busied herself pouring another mug of coffee.

"You wish what, honey?" Velda asked.

Ava wished she had the courage her mother had. That's what she'd been about to say. But she'd stopped herself. She wasn't sure she could talk about Bowie and his marriage proposal. Not without breaking down completely.

"Nothing. I just want you and Dad to be happy." Her voice choked on the last words, causing her mother to frown with concern.

"Ava, what's wrong?"

"Oh, Mom, I—" Before she could go on, tears suddenly fell from her eyes, and she quickly reached for a paper towel and dabbed at the moisture on her cheeks.

Velda crossed the few steps to her daughter and curled a comforting arm around her shoulders. "Ava, are you sad that I'm moving away? Because—"

"Hey, is there anything to eat in here?"

At the sound of the booming male voice, both women looked around to see Stu entering the kitchen. The sight of her tall, handsome father had Ava running to him and burying her face against his chest.

"Oh, my little girl," he crooned while gently patting her back. "What is this all about? Are you upset that your parents married again and I'm taking your mother down to San Diego?"

"I'm going to miss having Mom close by, but that's okay. I know you'll take care of her." Sniffing, she eased away from him and forced a smile, albeit a wobbly one.

"Forgive me for being so emotional. I came over here to have a nice visit with my parents and instead end up acting like a crybaby."

"Work, that's the problem, isn't it?" Velda asked knowingly. "You had some patients die on Christmas Day?"

No, Ava had died on Christmas Day, she thought. Ever since Bowie had walked out, she hadn't seen him or heard from him, and the days and nights without him had been some of the worst she'd ever been through in her life.

"It's not work," she admitted. "At least not the ER. But it does have something to do with a patient." With a regretful wail, she sank wearily into a chair. "I've fallen in love with him."

"Hallelujah, it's about time!" Velda exclaimed.

Stu's reaction was a far more gentle, "Aw, that's great, sweetie."

"No. It's not great," Ava mumbled. "Things didn't work out with him."

Her parents swooped around her chair.

"But why?" Velda demanded.

At the same time Stu patted her shoulder in an effort to console her. "That's too bad. But if you love him, maybe there's still a chance."

Shaking her head, Ava wiped at the foolish tears that continued to roll down her cheeks. "Bowie is a member of the BLM hotshot crew. He was seriously injured fighting a wildfire down in Texas. In fact, he was lucky to survive."

"So that's how you met," Velda said thoughtfully. "I think I recall you mentioning that you were going to care for a firefighter. Didn't you say he was a Calhoun?"

Before Ava could answer, Stu was staring incredulously at his wife. "You mean the Calhouns that own the Silver Horn?"

"That's right," Ava answered both questions, then glanced at her father. "Do you know them?"

"Actually, I do. When I still lived here in Carson City, Bart and Orin hired me to make some investments for them. If I remember right, Bart bought into a copper mine. And Orin put some money into a company that made medications for livestock. My God, the Calhouns have money to burn!"

Ava pressed her fingertips against her aching forehead. "Dad, their money has nothing to do with any of this. I don't care if Bowie is as poor as a snake or as rich as a king. I just can't deal with his career."

"Maybe you'd better back up a bit, Ava," her mother said. "You said you'd fallen in love, but you haven't told us how this man feels about you. Did things get serious between you two or was this a one-sided deal?"

Ava got to her feet. "Excuse me a minute," she told her parents. "There's something in my purse that I need to show you."

With her parents staring worriedly after her, Ava left the kitchen. By the time she'd returned carrying the satin pouch with the ring inside, they were both sitting down as though they were expecting even more shocking news from their daughter.

"Ava, are you pregnant? Is that what all these tears are about?" Velda asked quickly.

"I don't think so." The implications of her reply must have stunned her parents. Both of them remained quiet as Ava pulled the ring from its pouch and held it up for them to view. "Bowie gave me this ring for Christmas and asked me to marry him. I—I had to refuse."

Velda gasped. "But why, Ava? You've been alone for so long. And if you love the man—"

"I can't spend my days and nights worrying if my husband is going to come home to me in one piece, or at all," Ava explained. "I can't deal with that sort of life again."

Stu plucked the ring from Ava's fingers and whistled as he took a closer look. "Wow! I hate to admit this, Velda, but I'll never be able to buy you a hunk of stones like this."

"Daddy! Does it always come down to money with you?"

Rather than be offended, her father chuckled. "Sorry, honey. But men just naturally have an ego thing. We like to think we can give our women what they want. And we like to think we're seen as strong and brave providers."

"That's caveman mentality," Ava accused.

"Probably," Stu agreed. "But it's a psyche thing. And some things never change. Including you women putting up with our vanities." To prove his point, he leaned over and smacked a kiss on Velda's cheek. "Thanks, darling, for putting up with mine."

The affectionate exchange between her parents had Ava remembering back a few weeks ago when she'd bemoaned the fact that her parents were wasting so much precious time by living apart. They'd done something to fix the problem. But right now, Ava didn't see any way she could possibly fix hers.

"Ava, you say Bowie gave you this ring for Christmas," Velda said. "What did you give him? Besides a big *no*?"

"A pair of nice cowboy boots. That was all I could afford."

"Well, that's the problem right there," Velda said. "You

gave him the wrong gift. You should have given him a bubble."

Frowning with confusion, Ava stared at her mother. "What are you talking about?"

"You know, a bubble, to keep him safe and sound whenever he leaves the house."

Ava's mouth formed an outraged O, and Stu shot his wife a look of warning.

"Velda, the girl feels bad enough as it is," he scolded lightly. "Why don't you give her some advice that might help matters?"

"I just gave her the best advice a mother could give her daughter. But I doubt she'll listen. For the past thirteen years she's been determined to keep herself on a lonely, narrow path."

"That was advice?" Stu asked mockingly.

"Yes. And Ava knows exactly what I mean." Clearly disgusted, Velda looked at her husband. "Our daughter is never going to marry again. She's never going to give us grandchildren. And you know why? Because she's never going to find a man who can sign a guarantee that he won't be killed. She doesn't understand that any of us could die at any given moment. No matter what sort of job we have or how reckless we live. Just look at you, Stu. You might fall over any second with a heart attack, but that didn't stop me from marrying you a second time."

Stu jokingly pressed a hand to the middle of his chest. "My God, where are my car keys? I'd better get over to the ER quick and get my heart checked."

Ava bleakly shook her head. "Okay, you two, I get the point."

Her mother looked hopeful. "Do you really, darling?"

"I do," she mumbled miserably. "But that doesn't

mean— How can I get past this fear I have? When I think of Bowie going back into that kind of danger, I get ice-cold inside."

"And how do you feel inside at this moment?" Velda persisted. "All warm and good? You don't have to worry about a fire taking Bowie from you, dear Ava. Your incessant fears have already done that."

Stu reached for Ava's hand and pushed the ring onto her engagement finger. "The way your old dad sees it, you need to go tell this guy that all you want is him. The rest will take care of itself."

Ava looked down at the ring on her finger. She'd been carrying it with her for days now and asking herself why she didn't have the courage to put it on, to go to Bowie and show him she was ready for them to make a life together.

Ava's doubtful gaze swung from her mother's hopeful face to her father's confident smile. "I'm not sure that Bowie would believe me now—or even trust me. I said some awful things to him."

Stu's smile turned to one of understanding as he cast a loving look at Velda. "Your mother and I have said some pretty awful things to each other, too. But love has a way of erasing those things. Doesn't it, honey?"

"Love has magical powers," Velda agreed.

*Magical powers.* The two words caused hope to flicker deep inside Ava and she whispered wondrously to herself, "Like Christmas."

"What did you say?" Velda asked.

"I said Christmas really is a time for miracles." Ava jumped to her feet and kissed both her mother and father on the cheek. "I love you two. I'll see you later."

Grabbing up her handbag, she started out of the kitchen in a run.

"But what about helping us pack?" Stu called after her.

"Sorry," she called back to him. "I've got to go see about getting myself engaged."

## Chapter Eleven

Bowie was on his way out of the horse barn when he ran into Rafe.

"What are you doing?" Bowie asked him. "I thought you'd left for that cattlemen's meeting over in Ely."

"They postponed it. Bad weather is supposed to move in this afternoon." He gestured down the alleyway of the barn to where the new stallion was stalled. "I came by to take another look at Blue Dash. He's pretty special, isn't he?"

"A powerhouse," Bowie agreed.

"Come on, let's go take a look," Rafe told him.

Bowie fell into step beside his brother. "Dad and I just came from Blue's stall."

Rafe peered toward the far end of the large barn. "I don't see Dad anywhere. Has he already left the barn?"

"Colley called him over to the foaling barn."

Rafe glanced over at him. "Hope there wasn't a problem with one of the babies."

"No. I think he was all excited about a new colt that had just been born and wanted Dad to come take a look."

"And you didn't want to go with him?"

"I'm not much in the celebrating mood," Bowie admitted. "I'll look at the colt later."

They reached the stallion's stall and Bowie stood by his brother's side as the two men looked over the tall wire-mesh gate at the big steel-gray horse. At the moment, the animal was munching contentedly at the alfalfa hanging from a mesh holder.

"Oh, man, he's going to make some fine babies," Rafe commented. "Did Dad tell you that Finn found him for us?"

"No. He just said the horse came from California. I'd taken it for granted that Dad had located him."

"Give Finn the credit. He'd gone over to a ranch in Redding to see about buying a mustang and while he was there he spotted Blue and thought he'd be perfect for the Silver Horn."

Bowie sighed. "I wish Finn lived closer."

"Yeah. Me, too. But Finn is happy now. He's doing exactly what he wants to do. With the woman he loves by his side and a second baby on the way. Can life get any more perfect than that?"

Thoughts of Ava caused Bowie's chest to ache. "I wouldn't know."

Rafe was quiet for long moments and then he turned away from Blue's stall. "Let's go down to Finn's old office. Dad usually keeps some coffee and doughnuts in there."

"I'm not hungry."

Losing patience, Rafe asked, "Is it okay with you if I eat?"

"Sure. You go ahead. I need to get back to the house."

"What for? Haven't you spent enough time in that damned house?"

Bowie sighed. "Not the past few days. You and Dad seemed to be finding all sorts of little chores for me to do around the ranch."

"And you've enjoyed it, too. Don't try to tell me otherwise."

Bowie had to admit his brother was right. The more he worked around the ranch, intermingling with the hands and dealing with the livestock, the more Bowie was beginning to feel at home. He hadn't expected to have those sorts of feelings and he could only wonder what was causing the change in him. Had losing Ava caused something to shift in his thinking? Or was this the first time in his adult life that he'd allowed himself to take a closer look at the ranch he called home?

"Okay. I have rather liked it," he admitted as he followed Rafe into the rustic room that served as a small office. "Especially feeding the twins their bottles. I've grown attached to those two little bull calves."

Inside the room, Rafe pointed to a leather chair behind the desk. "You take the office chair. You're the one with the gimpy leg."

"You take it. I'll sit right here. Gimpy leg and all." Bowie took a seat in a straight-backed wooden chair and propped his foot on an empty feed bucket.

Rafe poured a foam cup full of coffee and carried it and a doughnut over to the desk, where he ignored the chair and sat on the front of the desktop.

"So what did you get me in here for?" Bowie asked

bluntly. "To give me a lecture about going to work for the ranch?"

"No. I probably should. I mean, this is where you're meant to be. But I don't want to get you all stirred up about that right now. I wanted to talk to you about something else."

Surprised, Bowie looked at his brother. Rafe was one lean, tough piece of rawhide, and Bowie figured if for some reason the two of them ever came to physical blows, it would be a toss-up as to which one would come out the winner. Yet it wasn't only Rafe's physical strength that Bowie admired, it was also his mental strength. Clancy might be the ranch manager, but it was Rafe, the foreman, who was the true heart and soul of the Silver Horn. He not only kept the men going, he made them want to ride for the brand.

"And what is that?" Bowie asked.

"Ava."

Bowie stiffened. So far, none of his family had said much about the abrupt end of Ava's visits, except Grandfather Bart. He'd wanted to know why the pretty nurse wasn't around anymore and Bowie had simply explained to the older man that he no longer needed medical care.

"What about her?"

Rafe let out an impatient groan. "Oh, come on, Bowie. Do you think I'm an idiot? The whole family could see you were getting close to her. From what Greta tells me, you had Christmas dinner with the woman. And now she no longer comes to the ranch and you're behaving as though you've been sentenced to a lifetime of agony."

That's the sentence Ava had handed out to him when she'd refused his marriage proposal, Bowie thought. Without her, he was only half a man, his life incomplete.

Grimacing, Bowie looked away from his brother. "I've done a fool thing, Rafe. Something I thought I wouldn't do for a long time to come."

"What's that?"

"I fell in love and asked a woman to marry me."

A shocked breath whooshed out of Rafe. "Ava?"

Unable to hide his frustration, Bowie snapped, "Who the hell have we been talking about?"

"I know we've been talking about Ava. But I didn't— I thought she was just a girlfriend and you were bent out of shape because she wasn't coming around anymore. After all," he added shrewdly, "you've had plenty of girl-friends over the years."

"You had plenty of them, too—before you married Lilly."

"Good point," Rafe muttered. "But that's all behind me. And I'm not sure you're ready for marriage. I sure don't see it working very well with you running all over the place fighting fires."

Closing his eyes, Bowie wiped a weary hand over his face. "Well, no need to worry about having a divorce in the family, big brother. Ava turned me down. So there isn't going to be a marriage. Not for me."

"And her reason? She doesn't love you?"

The tiny ache that had started in the middle of Bowie's chest a few moments ago had continued to spread. Now the pain was so big it was practically choking him.

"Oh, she said she loved me," he mumbled. "But that's hard to believe when in the same breath she says she can't marry me—because I work on the hotshot crew."

"Hmm. And you told her that being a firefighter is more important to you than her."

Bowie scowled at him. "I didn't say it like that. But

I did explain that it was my job and it was important to me. It isn't right for her to be dictating what I should do with my future. You certainly wouldn't have walked away from your job just for Lilly."

"I'd do anything for Lilly. And she'd do anything for me. Fortunately, she wouldn't ask me to do something that would make me unhappy. And I wouldn't ask her to do anything that would cause her misery."

Unable to remain still, Bowie got to his feet and began to move restlessly around the small room. The space was full of dust and shadows, as though it had been neglected. Just like his heart, he thought wretchedly.

"Then you're lucky as hell, brother."

Rafe remained silent for long moments and then he said, "You need to remember that Ava is a widow. Now that she's found love again, she's bound to be a bit overprotective. She's afraid she'll lose you."

"And how am I supposed to deal with that? She's being unreasonable."

"Who ever said that love made sense?" Rafe countered.

Bowie blew out a lungful of air. "So tell me, Rafe, what would you do?"

Rafe shook his head. "I can't tell you what to do. But I can tell you what I did."

Turning away from a tall, dusty file cabinet, Bowie looked at his brother. "What does that mean?"

Rafe let out a short laugh. "Do you think my courtship with Lilly was all smooth sailing? I went through hell trying to persuade her to marry me. For a while there I even began to believe she hated me. But in the end I refused to let her go. So I'm telling you, Bowie, if you really love Ava, you won't give up on her. You'll keep trying. Again and again."

*Why are you worrying about things going wrong instead of being happy that your parents are brave enough to try again?*

The words he'd said to Ava on Christmas Day suddenly drifted through Bowie's mind and he realized she wasn't the only one who needed to find an extra dose of courage. He needed to follow his own advice and find enough backbone to go to her, to make her see that if her parents were brave enough to marry again, then she could be, too.

He cast a cautious but hopeful look at Rafe. "You're right, Rafe. I can't give up."

Rafe smiled knowingly. "Now you're talking like my feisty little brother."

Motivated with hope, Bowie shoved up the cuffs of his shirt and glanced at his watch. "It's still a few hours before Ava's evening shift starts," he said. "If I leave now, I'll have plenty of time to talk to her before she goes to work."

"Don't waste time telling me. Get gone," Rafe told him.

Bowie started out of the office but nearly ran straight into Denver, Rafe's right-hand man. At the same time behind him, Bowie could hear his brother's phone begin to ring.

"Oh, sorry, Bowie! I was hunting Rafe," he said between gasps for air. "All hell has broken loose!"

Rafe hurried forward. "What's happened?"

The tough cowboy looked at both men as though he couldn't believe they were so clueless.

"Didn't you hear any commotion? You're not that far from Blue's stall."

"We haven't heard anything." Rafe looked at Bowie. "Tell him."

"Not a sound," Bowie told him. "Other than one little nicker from one of the horses on this end of the barn."

Denver looked even more shocked. "That's crazy! Blue is out of his stall and gone! And he's taken a pasture full of mares with him! Some of the hands saw the whole herd racing out of the ranch yard—toward the west range."

With a murderous expression, Rafe started out the door. Denver and Bowie followed close on his heels as the three men hurried toward the stallion's stall.

Rafe barked, "We would've heard him kicking down the stall gate. Was it broken?"

"I haven't looked yet," Denver admitted. "I've been hunting you. I rang your cell, but you didn't answer."

Rafe cursed under his breath. "The ringer was accidentally turned off. I just discovered it about the time you burst into the office."

By now they'd reached the stallion's stall and Bowie stared in stunned fascination at the wide-open gate. There was no damage to it or the latch, proving that a human had committed the act.

"The gate was fastened firmly when we were here," Bowie said harshly. "That was less than a half hour ago. Somebody opened it! Some bastard around here let him out!"

Rafe shot Denver a livid glance. "What about the mares? How did they get out?"

"I sent Randy and Tom over to check the fences and gates. I should hear from them any minute. What are we going to do now?" Denver asked. "Should I tell the men to saddle up?"

"Hell yes," Rafe barked. "We've got to get that stallion back. He's running wild over ground he's never been over before. He could do all sorts of damage to himself. And I don't even want to think about him and those mares connecting up with a band of mustangs. There'd be a hell of a fight with those stallions. And the mares—well, they'd be lost!"

"I'll be at the saddling barn," Denver told him, then took off in a jog.

Rafe turned urgently to Bowie. "Tell everyone at the house what's happened. I may be gone all night."

Bowie shook his head. "I'm not going to the house. I'm going with you."

"No. You're in no shape. Besides, you're going to see Ava."

Rafe started out of the barn, and even though Bowie was still limping somewhat, he was able to maintain his brother's quick strides.

"Ava will hopefully understand—about a lot of things. I'll see her as soon as we get back. Right now you need every hand you have for this job," Bowie argued. "I can keep up. No, I can do more than keep up. I can help."

Rafe paused in midstride. "You think so?"

Bowie's jaw tightened with determination. "I'll show you."

Rafe started to slap him on the shoulder, but at the last second remembered it was still healing. "Then come on. We don't have time to waste."

As they hurried out of the barn and across the ranch yard, Bowie questioned his brother. "Rafe, who do you think did this? Why would anyone want to cause us this much harm? To cause the horses harm?"

"I don't have a clue," he said gravely. "But we're going to find out. Even if we have to get Evan out here on official business!"

Ava noticed the ranch yard appeared eerily empty as she drove to the back of the house and parked her car. Normally in the late afternoon, the barns and lots were buzzing with cowboys moving loads of feed and hay. What could be going on, she wondered. Where was everyone?

When Greta opened the door to let her into the kitchen, the older woman gasped with relief and practically jerked her over the threshold.

"Thank God, you're here, Ava!" the cook exclaimed. "It's awful. Just awful."

Uneasiness swept through her. "What's awful? What's happened? When I drove up I didn't see a soul around the ranch yard."

"That's because they're all out. Except for Bart, that is. And he's upstairs cursing and snorting because Orin wouldn't let him saddle up. The damned old man. He ought to know he can't chase after a stallion! Not at his age!"

"Stallion? Greta, I don't understand. Slow down, back up and explain what's happened."

While Ava removed her coat and hung it on a hall tree, Greta plopped into a chair at the end of the breakfast table and frantically wiped a hand across her brow.

"Orin and Bart purchased a new stallion for the ranch. The horse only got here yesterday and they had him stalled inside the horse barn. From what Rafe explained over the phone to Lilly, someone let him out. Now he's run off to God only knows where. Not only that, but a bunch of prize mares were let out with him."

Greta's news left Ava weak in the knees, and she sank into the chair next to the cook.

"Oh, that is awful," she murmured as all sorts of thoughts and questions began to swirl in her head. "So that's where all the men have gone? They're trying to round up the mares and stallion?"

"That's right. And it'll be dark soon. I'm not a cowgirl, but I know how dangerous it is to ride the range in the dark. Anything can happen."

Ava swallowed as a sense of doom threatened to overwhelm her. "What about Bowie? Where is he?"

"He's out with his brother. The fool. The boy just gets to where he can walk again and he goes and climbs on a horse. The next thing he breaks might be his neck!"

"Don't say that, Greta!" Ava gently scolded.

The cook looked at her and groaned. "I'm sorry, Ava. I'm rattling on because I'm damned mad. Someone on this ranch meant to do some damage—to the horses and the men!"

The notion was almost too incredible for Ava to comprehend. "When did this happen, Greta?"

"Two or three hours ago. I'm not sure. We didn't hear about it here at the house until later."

Ava had been late driving here to the ranch because she'd had trouble trying to locate a nurse willing to work her shift tonight. Perhaps if she'd been here earlier, when the horses had gone missing, she could've persuaded Bowie to stay here on the ranch where he would've been safe. Instead, he was out there roaming around in the mountains and gullies, where his horse could step in a hole or trip on a rock or fallen log.

*Listen to yourself, Ava. You want to treat Bowie as if he's a baby that needs protecting, instead of a strong, brave man capable of taking care of himself. What do you want? To make a wimp out of him? Would that make you happy?*

The voice going off in her head jolted Ava, then just as suddenly a calmness settled over her. And she knew, with more certainty than she'd ever felt in her life, that she wanted Bowie to be her husband, no matter what job he chose for himself. That would make her happy. Now her only concern was whether he'd forgive her for being so blind and obstinate.

She looked over at the harried cook. "Don't worry, Greta. The men are skilled riders and they know what they're doing. I'm sure everything will be all right," she told her, then marveled at how good it felt to be positive.

Greta nodded, then rose to her feet. "You're right. I need to quit worrying. And I'm not being a very good hostess. Would you like coffee or something?"

"No, thanks. Maybe later. Is Lilly here?"

"She's upstairs with the little ones."

Ava got to her feet. "I'll go see how she's doing. She might need some help with the kids."

Out at Salt Cedar Flats, on a river trail northwest of the ranch, Bowie and Rafe were traveling their horses in a long trot while searching for tracks as best they could in the darkness. After hours in the saddle, the two brothers had broken away from the rest of the group on a hunch that the stallion might have taken a notion to head toward the mountains. Orin and Denver had remained on the White Pine Range, where the men had found a few of the scattered mares and were busy rounding them up.

"If there are any mustangs on the place they'll be on the backside of Eagle's Ridge," Rafe said. "And for some reason, I have a suspicion Blue headed in that direction."

Bowie tugged the brim of his cowboy hat down lower on his forehead in an effort to block out the snowflakes pelting him directly in the face. About twenty minutes ago, the weather had taken a turn for the worse and now the wind was howling and threatening to pound the whole range with blizzard conditions.

"What makes you think that?" Bowie asked, raising his voice above the sound of the wind. "You'd think he would stay with the mares."

"I have a feeling some of the mares, the ones in season, are probably with him. And he's going to take them to a place where he thinks nothing will threaten him or his harem. The north side of Eagle's Ridge is rough, but there's a deep gorge below that would give them shelter."

"Blue wouldn't know that," Bowie argued.

"Animal instinct. They know where to go to survive."

"I've got a lot to learn yet about ranching."

In spite of the snow and the darkness, Rafe looked in his direction. "Do you want to learn?"

Bowie reined his spotted mount alongside Rafe's gray horse, Gunsmoke. "More than anything," he told his brother.

Rafe angled his head so that the snow was hitting the crown of his hat rather than his face. "What's brought that on?"

"I think tonight, for the first time in my life, I realized that you and Dad need me."

Rafe grinned. "Oh, hell, Bowie, we've always needed you. You just couldn't see it."

With a lump in his throat, Bowie said, "Come on, let's pick up the pace. If I remember right, the trail to Eagle's Ridge isn't far. And we're not going to find Blue down here. Lead the way."

The two men kicked the horses into a short lope and for the next couple of minutes rode side by side along the riverbank until they reached a bend. To the right of it, a cattle trail led up an embankment. Bowie and Rafe made the turn and started the steep climb up the mountain.

"There," Bowie shouted after a moment. "I see a few tracks and they're leading upward. Let's go!"

The trail turned to switchbacks with Rafe leading the way. The ground was rocky and the snow made everything slick. Bowie was concentrating on leaning up in the saddle to aid his horse in making the climb when suddenly in front of him, Gunsmoke took a wrong step and stumbled.

Bowie watched in horror as the horse tried to gather his footing, but fell backward instead. In a split second, Bowie jumped his horse out of the way as Gunsmoke rolled off the trail and onto his side. The spill slung Rafe from the saddle and landed him against the twisted trunk of a half-dead juniper.

"Rafe!" Jumping from the saddle, Bowie hurried over to his fallen brother. "Are you hurt?"

To his relief, Rafe groaned and attempted to push himself to a sitting position. "I—I just need some air. Gunsmoke—is he all right?"

"Don't try to get up yet. I'll look after the horse."

Knowing Rafe considered Gunsmoke his child, Bowie sent up a prayer of thanks when he found the animal on his feet. After making a hasty inspection, he led the horse over to where his brother was still sitting hunched over and struggling to catch his breath.

"Here he is," Bowie told him. "He's got a cut on his hind leg. I don't think it's serious. But if I were you I wouldn't risk riding him any farther."

"I don't intend to," Rafe said. "He's too special to take the chance of crippling him."

Bowie tethered Gunsmoke's reins to a nearby limb, then squatted on his heels in front of his brother. "Rafe, do you think you've broken a rib? You might have punctured a lung."

"No. It's not that bad. I'm getting my breath back now. I just whammed the ground so hard it knocked the air from me."

Relief swept over Bowie. At least his brother didn't believe he was seriously injured. "So what now? Will this horse of mine ride double?"

"It doesn't matter whether he will or not. I'm staying put." To make his point, he scooted under the juniper limb to shelter himself from the snow. "You go on after the stallion. Some of the hands will probably come this way looking for us eventually. Don't worry about me."

Bowie hated to leave Rafe behind, but there was a fire in his belly to catch the stallion. And getting Blue Dash back before the horse was lost to a herd of mustangs would help Rafe far more than a ride back to the ranch.

He untied a weatherproof bedroll from the back of Rafe's saddle and wrapped it around his brother's shoulders. "I'll be back as soon as I can."

Rafe gave him a thumbs-up and Bowie swung himself onto the paint's back and hurried up the snowy mountain trail.

\* \* \*

In the family room Ava and Lilly stared through the wall of glass that allowed them a partial view of the ranch yard. Several hours had passed since Ava had arrived and they hadn't seen any sort of movement down at the barns or heard a word from the men.

"The snow is getting worse," Lilly said. "Between that and the darkness, I don't know how the men can see anything. How can they tell a horse from a Joshua tree?"

"I was wondering the same thing. And the temperature has to be dropping rapidly." Ava turned away from the window and forced herself to take a seat on the couch. "This is like working the ER shift. You never know what kind of emergency is going to come through the doors, or when."

Her arms wrapped around her middle, Lilly gave her a wan smile. "I'm glad you're here, Ava. At least we can wait together."

Little Colleen and baby Austin had been put to bed hours ago, and Tessa had insisted on staying in the nursery so that Lilly could come downstairs. Since then Ava and Lilly had been pacing the family room, waiting and hoping to hear some sort of news.

Footsteps suddenly sounded in the doorway and both women jerked their heads in that direction. Since Greta rarely left her domain in the kitchen, it was apparent the cook had some sort of information to share.

Lilly moved anxiously toward Greta and Ava rose to her feet to join them.

"What is it, Greta?" Lilly asked.

"Orin just called the kitchen phone. He and Rafe have made it back. But Bowie is still out on the mountain, searching for the stallion."

Trying not to panic, Ava went to stand close to Lilly's side and directed her question to the cook. "Why would Rafe and Orin come back and leave Bowie to keep searching?"

Greta made a helpless gesture with her hands. "Orin only gave me bits and pieces of information. He said something about Rafe taking a bad spill and that Bowie went on without him. Guess we'll find out more when the men get here to the house. I'm going back to the kitchen to make coffee and sandwiches. I figure it's going to be a long night."

The woman hurried away, leaving Ava and Lilly to exchange anxious glances.

"I can't believe this is happening," Ava said hoarsely. "I drove out here to the ranch to tell Bowie I was over worrying about him returning to the hotshot crew—that I could deal with whatever job he chose for himself. Now here he is being a cowboy—something I thought would be safe—but I can see the job is far, far from it. How ironic is that?"

Lilly wrapped a comforting arm around Ava's shoulders. "Calhoun men don't shrink from danger," she said. "If you love Bowie, it's something you'll accept. And you do love him, don't you?"

Ava didn't hesitate to answer. "I love him very much."

Lilly gave her an understanding smile. "Come on," she gently urged. "Let's go to the kitchen and help Greta. Like she said, it might be a long night."

It didn't matter how long or agonizing the night turned out to be, Ava thought as she followed her friend through the opulent ranch house. She'd stay until she saw Bowie again. Until she convinced him that he was the only thing that mattered in her life.

## Chapter Twelve

By the time Bowie finally got back to the ranch, it was nearing two o'clock in the morning. He was cold and wet and dog tired, but as he trudged his way up to the house, he felt a true sense of accomplishment.

The stallion was back in his stall, skinned and scuffed in places, but safe and sound. He hadn't been easy to catch, but after several attempts Bowie had managed to get a rope on him. Once that was accomplished, it had been a matter of leading him back over Eagle's Ridge to a point where he could be loaded into a trailer and hauled back to the ranch.

Inside the house, a night-light was on in the kitchen. Bowie found a plate of sandwiches wrapped in cellophane and a thermos of coffee sitting on the counter. He plucked up three of the sandwiches and the thermos and carried the whole lot with him as he limped his way through the house and up the staircase to his bedroom.

He wasn't sure what he wanted first—a hot shower to warm him or the food to ease the gnawing ache in his stomach. But as soon as he opened the bedroom door, flipped on the overhead light and spotted Ava lying on his bed, both options were completely forgotten.

The sudden glare of the light must have woken her, because she sat straight up and blinked in confusion. Bowie stared in stunned fascination at the woman who'd come to be his very life. What was she doing here?

"Bowie," she said with soft amazement. "You're home."

Still carrying the sandwiches and thermos, Bowie walked over to the bed and placed them on the nightstand. "No one told me you were here," he said stiffly. "Why did you come? You heard about the emergency and thought I'd need nursing again?"

Bowie realized he sounded bitter, but he couldn't help it. When she'd refused to marry him it had squashed his heart and his pride.

"When I drove out here this afternoon I didn't know about the horses or you going after them. Not until Greta told me."

He cut a sharp glance at her. "This afternoon? You've been here since then?"

She nodded. "I came to see you. But you'd already left to go after the stallion."

"To see me?" he repeated with amazement. "Why? I thought you didn't want anything else to do with me. I'm a firefighter, remember? I might get myself killed just to spoil your life again."

"Oh, Bowie, I'm sorry," she said quietly. "That's why I drove out here to the ranch. To tell you I'd been wrong about you—about us."

Unsure that he was hearing her right, he turned and slowly studied her face. "Wrong? Are you saying—"

Before he could finish, she closed the small space between them and with a muffled groan wrapped her arms around his waist.

"I'm saying I love you. I want to be your wife. I don't care if you stay on the hotshot crew, carry a badge and gun like Evan or become a car salesman. I want us to be together—for as long as God allows."

When the gist of her words finally settled in his weary brain, joy rushed through him and with it came a wave of excitement and energy.

Chuckling softly, he said, "I'm not sure about the car salesman, Ava—that's a pretty risky vocation. People get mighty angry when they're given a low trade-in price."

She began to laugh, too, and as happiness overtook him, he swept her into the circle of his arms and buried his face in the curve of her neck.

"Oh, Ava, I love you. I've never stopped loving you." He eased her head back far enough to look into her eyes. "But how—what caused you to change your mind?"

"Spending the past ten days without you has been a nightmare, Bowie. I've known all along that I needed to change, to shake off my past. Loving you has finally given me the courage to do that. Along with a little nudge from my parents. I saw them today. They're married again and Mom's packing to go live with Dad down in San Diego."

"Does that make you sad?"

"No, it makes me happy. Just like it's going to make me happy whenever we become man and wife."

"And that can't be soon enough for me," he said, then, bending his head, he placed a long, lengthy kiss on her lips. One that promised nights of passion and a lifetime of love. "Do you still have the ring I gave you?"

Lifting her left hand, she revealed the ruby and diamond ring encircling her finger. "Even before I drove out here, I had already decided this is the hand it belonged on."

Certain he was standing on air, Bowie lifted her hand to his lips and kissed the soft skin. "I have a confession to make, Ava. This afternoon, before the incident with the horses, I had decided to drive into town to see you and somehow convince you that we were meant to be together. I wanted to tell you that being a firefighter didn't mean nearly as much to me as you, my darling."

Joyous tears misted her eyes as she looked up at him. "Oh, Bowie, I don't want you to make that kind of sacrifice for me. Like I just told you, I can live with any career you choose."

"Even being a cowboy here on the ranch?"

Her eyes grew wide. "Are you serious?"

"Absolutely."

"But you called it boring. You wanted to do something where you could make a difference."

His hands roamed her back as the warmth of her body began to awaken the need in his.

"You talked about struggling to shake off your past. Well, it finally dawned on me that I needed to do the same thing. You were right when you said I'd been running away from myself. But tonight I decided to quit running. And you know what? It felt damned good. I realized I'm no longer the little brother tagging along, trying to compete with my big brothers. I'm all grown up and I can give just as much to the ranch as they can. My contributions might be different than Rafe's or Clancy's, but that's the way it should be."

A beaming smile on her face, she said, "I think falling in love has taught us both a lot of things."

He stroked her hair, loving the texture of it beneath his fingers. "Yeah. And I expect it will keep on teaching us things for the rest of our lives."

She suddenly stepped back from him and eyed him up and down. "You look like you've been in a fight with a mountain lion! Tell me, what happened with the stallion and the mares? When Rafe and Orin came in without you, I didn't know what to think."

"It's a long story. But the stallion is back home. And I'll give you every detail later." His eyes twinkling, he stepped toward her. "Right now I'm wondering if you still remember how to give me a sponge bath."

Her lips curving into a wicked little smile, she reached for his hand. "Nurse Ava to the rescue."

## *Epilogue*

Bowie and Ava were married the following month on Valentine's Day. The wedding was held at the same church the Calhoun family had attended for the past eighty years. Although Ava hadn't had much time to prepare for any sort of elaborate wedding, Lilly and Paige helped her put together a simple yet beautiful ceremony.

Pink and red flowers filled the lovely old church with its worn pews and stained-glass windows. Wearing pale pink dresses, Paige served as Ava's one bridesmaid while Lilly stood as her matron of honor. As for Ava's dress, she'd chosen to wear champagne-colored lace over the same color taffeta. The full gathered skirt was ballerina length and the long fitted sleeves stopped at her wrist. The neckline was a modest scoop in the front, while the low dip in the back managed to give the elegant garment a sexy flair.

Bowie had asked Rafe to act as his best man, and

the two brothers looked extremely handsome in dark Western-cut suits and cowboy boots. Little Colleen was adorable as the flower girl, and Sassy's oldest son, J.J., managed to stand still long enough to be the ring bearer.

The church overflowed with family and friends, all of whom followed them to the Silver Horn, where a huge reception was held in the formal living room of the Calhoun ranch house.

Now as Bowie danced Ava around the floor to music supplied by a four-piece band, the champagne continued to flow while the tiered white cake was steadily being demolished.

"Look at this gang of people! Are they here because they wanted to see us married or for the free food and champagne?" Bowie asked, his expression one of comical amazement as he glanced around the packed room. "I never expected this big of a crowd, did you?"

Ava laughed softly. "No. But we shouldn't be surprised. With your father doing the guest list for you and my mother handling mine, we should've known they would go overboard. But I think it's lovely that so many people are here. And it's so special that all of our families are here. You got to meet my brother for the first time. I can tell Tray likes you."

"I liked him, too. He seems like a stand-up guy."

"He is. And speaking of stand-up guys, I really like your grandfather Tuck. He and your grandmother Alice seem like quite a pair. I hope we can go visit them soon."

"We'll make a point to," he promised, then added jokingly, "When I was a little boy, Grandpa Tuck never had any trouble keeping me in line. He'd just threaten to put me in jail if I didn't behave. And I believed him."

The mention of the retired sheriff had Ava's thoughts

shifting to last month's incident with the stallion and mares. Even though Evan was looking into the matter, so far no suspects had emerged in the investigation. For the most part no harm had come to Blue Dash or the herd of mares, and Orin had come to the conclusion that someone had merely let the horses out as a prank, albeit a bad one. Ava and Bowie didn't agree with Orin's assessment, but today they were keeping their opinions to themselves. It was their wedding day and they wanted to enjoy every moment of it.

In spite of that, the story of how Bowie had snagged the loose stallion and brought him down Eagle's Ridge had been told and retold. The ranch hands and everyone in the family considered him a hero for his efforts, but Bowie humbly insisted he'd only been doing a cowboy's job. A job that Ava could safely say her husband had already come to relish.

She smiled at his comment about his grandfather Tuck. "That's good to know. If you get out of line, I'll know who to call for help," Ava teased.

His eyes sparkled as he smiled at her. "Happy, Mrs. Calhoun?"

Her sigh was a note of pure joy. "If you weren't holding on to me, I'd probably float off the floor."

He chuckled. "Don't worry, darling. I'm not about to take my hands off you—not for a long, long while."

"So tell me, Mr. Calhoun, are you going to wake up tomorrow morning and regret you've lost your freedom?"

The playful light in his eyes turned serious. "I'm going to wake up in the morning with you in my arms and thank God that you're my wife."

"Oh, Bowie, I love you," she whispered, then nestled her head against his shoulder until the song ended.

It wasn't until later, after they'd left the dance floor and were sipping champagne in the most discreet area in the room they could find, that Ava asked, "Bowie, who is the woman who caught my bridal bouquet? She's standing over there by your sister, Sassy."

Bowie glanced across the crowded room to where a tall dark-haired woman stood next to his redheaded sister. "That's Bella Sundell. Sassy's sister-in-law."

"So she's the sister of Jett Sundell, the Silver Horn's lawyer," Ava mused aloud. "I've never met her before. She's lovely. Is she married?"

"No. So maybe the bouquet will work its charm for her."

"Hmm. Maybe when the magical time of Christmas comes again, she'll have a man propose to her like I did," she murmured slyly.

He smiled suggestively down at her. "And maybe by the time yuletide rolls around, we'll be celebrating a baby. I loved the boots you gave me, honey, but a son or daughter would be a mighty thrilling gift."

Her laughter full of love, she said, "We're going to have a two-week honeymoon to work on that project. Think you're up to the task?"

Curling his arm around her waist, he hugged her close and whispered in her ear. "A Calhoun always gets his job done. Merry Christmas, darling."

"Bowie, it's Valentine's Day," she gently corrected.

"Yes. But with you in my life, sweet Ava, it's Christmas every day of the year."

\* \* \* \* \*

SHE SIGHED. HE WAS very handsome. She loved the way his eyes crinkled when he smiled. She loved the strong, chiseled lines of his wide mouth, the high cheekbones, the thick black wavy hair around his leonine face. His chest was a work of art in itself. She had to force herself not to look at it too much. It was broad and muscular, under a thick mat of curling black hair that ran down to the waistband of his silk pajamas. Apparently, he didn't like jackets, because he never wore one with the bottoms. His arms were muscular, without being overly so. He would have delighted an artist.

"What are you thinking so hard about?" he wondered aloud.

"That an artist would love painting you," she blurted out, and then flushed then cleared her throat. "Sorry. I wasn't thinking."

He lifted both eyebrows. "Miss Ashton," he scoffed, "you aren't by any chance flirting with me, are you?"

"Mr. Coleman, the thought never crossed my mind!"

"Don't obsess over me," he said firmly, but his eyes were still twinkling. "I'm a married man."

She sighed. "Yes, thank goodness."

His eyebrows lifted in a silent question.

"Well, if you weren't married, I'd probably disgrace myself. Imagine, trying to ravish a sick man in bed because I'm obsessing over the way he looks without a shirt!"

He burst out laughing. "Go away, you bad girl."

Her own eyes twinkled. "I'll banish myself to the kitchen and make lovely things for you to eat."

"I'll look forward to that."

She smiled and left him.

He looked after her with conflicting emotions. He had a wife. Sadly, one who was a disappointment in almost every way; a cold woman who took and took without a thought of giving anything back. He'd married her thinking she was the image of his mother. Elise had seemed very different while they were dating. But the minute the ring was on her finger, she was off on her travels, spending more and more of his money, linking up with old friends whom she paid to travel with her. She was never home. In fact, she made a point of avoiding her husband as much as possible.

This really was the last straw, though, ignoring him when he was ill. It had cut him to the quick to have Todd and Niki see the emptiness of their relationship. He wasn't that sick. It was the principle of the thing. Well, he had some thinking to do when he left the Ashtons, didn't he?

CHRISTMAS DAY WAS BOISTEROUS. Niki and Edna and three other women took turns putting food on the table for an unending succession of people who worked for the Ashtons. Most were cowboys, but several were executives from Todd's oil corporation.

Niki liked them all, but she was especially fond of their children. She dreamed of having a child of her own one day. She spent hours in department stores, ogling the baby things.

She got down on the carpet with the children around the Christmas tree, oohing and aahing over the presents as they opened them. One little girl who was six years old got a Barbie doll with a holiday theme. The child cried when she opened the gaily wrapped package.

"Lisa, what's wrong, baby?" Niki cooed, drawing her into her lap.

"Daddy never buys me dolls, and I love dolls so much, Niki," she whispered. "Thank you!" She kissed Niki and held on tight.

"You should tell him that you like dolls, sweetheart," Niki said, hugging her close.

"I did. He bought me a big yellow truck."

"A what?"

"A truck, Niki," the child said with a very grown-up sigh. "He wanted a little boy. He said so."

Niki looked as indignant as she felt. But she forced herself to smile at the child. "I think little girls are very sweet," she said softly, brushing back the pretty dark hair.

"So do I," Blair said, kneeling down beside them. He smiled at the child, too. "I wish I had a little girl."

"You do? Honest?" Lisa asked, wide-eyed.

"Honest."

She got up from Niki's lap and hugged the big man. "You're nice."

He hugged her back. It surprised him, how much he wanted a child. He drew back, the smile still on his face. "So are you, precious."

"I'm going to show Mama my doll," she said. "Thanks, Niki!"

"You're very welcome."

The little girl ran into the dining room, where the adults were finishing dessert.

"Poor thing," Niki said under her breath. "Even if he thinks it, he shouldn't have told her."

"She's a nice child," he said, getting to his feet. He looked down at Niki. "You're a nice child, yourself."

She made a face at him. "Thanks. I think."

His dark eyes held an expression she'd never seen before. They fell to her waistline and jerked back up. He turned away. "Any more coffee going? I'm sure mine's cold."

"Edna will have made a new pot by now," she said. His attitude disconcerted her. Why had he looked at her that way? Her eyes followed him as he strode back into the dining room, towering over most of the other men. The little girl smiled up at him, and he ruffled her hair.

He wanted children. She could see it. But apparently his wife didn't. What a waste, she thought. What a wife he had. She felt sorry for him. He'd said when he was engaged that he was crazy about Elise. Why didn't she care enough to come when he was ill?

"It's not my business," she told herself firmly.

It wasn't. But she felt very sorry for him just the same. If he'd married *her*, they'd have a houseful of children. She'd take care of him and love him and nurse him when he was sick… She pulled herself up short. He was a married man. She shouldn't be thinking such things.

SHE'D BOUGHT PRESENTS online for her father and Edna and Blair. She was careful to get Blair something impersonal. She didn't want his wife to think she was chasing him or anything. She picked out a tie tack, a *fleur de lis* made of solid gold. She couldn't understand why she'd chosen such a thing. He had Greek ancestry, as far as she knew, not French. It had been an impulse.

Her father had gone to answer the phone, a call from a business associate who wanted to wish him happy holidays, leaving Blair and Niki alone in the living room by the tree. She felt like an idiot for making the purchase.

Now Blair was opening the gift, and she ground her teeth together when he took the lid off the box and stared at it with wide, stunned eyes.

"I'm sorry," she began self-consciously. "The sales slip is in there," she added. "You can exchange it if…"

He looked at her. His expression stopped her tirade midsentence. "My mother was French," he said quietly. "How did you know?"

She faltered. She couldn't manage words. "I didn't. It was an impulse."

His big fingers smoothed over the tie tac. "In fact, I had one just like it that she bought me when I graduated from college." He swallowed. Hard. "Thanks."

"You're very welcome."

His dark eyes pinned hers. "Open yours now."

She fumbled with the small box he'd had hidden in his suitcase until this morning. She tore off the ribbons and opened it. Inside was the most beautiful brooch she'd ever seen. It was a golden orchid on an ivory background. The orchid was purple with a yellow center, made of delicate amethyst and topaz and gold.

She looked at him with wide, soft eyes. "It's so beautiful…"

He smiled with real affection. "It reminded me of you, when I saw it in the jewelry store," he lied, because he'd had it commissioned by a noted jewelry craftsman, just for her. "Little hothouse orchid," he teased.

She flushed. She took the delicate brooch out of its box and pinned it to the bodice of her black velvet dress. "I've never had anything so lovely," she faltered. "Thank you."

He stood up and drew her close to him. "Thank you, Niki." He bent and started to brush her mouth with his, but forced himself to deflect the kiss to her soft cheek. "Merry Christmas."

She felt the embrace to the nails of her toes. He smelled of expensive cologne and soap, and the feel of that powerful body so close to hers made her vibrate inside. She was flustered by the contact, and uneasy because he was married.

She laughed, moving away. "I'll wear it to church every Sunday," she promised without really looking at him.

He cleared his throat. The contact had affected him, too. "I'll wear mine to board meetings, for a lucky charm," he teased gently. "To ward off hostile takeovers."

"I promise it will do the job," she replied, and grinned.

Her father came back to the living room, and the sudden, tense silence was broken. Conversation turned to politics and the weather, and Niki joined in with forced cheerfulness.

But she couldn't stop touching the orchid brooch she'd pinned to her dress.

Time passed. Blair's visits to the ranch had slowed until they were almost nonexistent. Her father said Blair was trying to make his marriage work. Niki thought, privately, that it would take a miracle to turn fun-loving Elise into a housewife. But she forced herself not to dwell on it. Blair was married. Period. She did try to go out more with her friends, but never on a blind date again. The experience with Harvey had affected her more than she'd realized.

Graduation day came all too soon. Niki had enjoyed college. The daily commute was a grind, especially in the harsh winter, but thanks to Tex, who could drive in snow and ice, it was never a problem. Her grade point average was good enough for a magna cum laude award. And she'd already purchased her class ring months before.

"Is Blair coming with Elise, do you think?" Niki asked her father as they parted inside the auditorium just before the graduation ceremony.

He looked uncomfortable. "I don't think so," he said. "They've had some sort of blowup," he added. "Blair's butler, Jameson, called me last night. He said Blair locked himself in his study and won't come out."

"Oh, dear," Niki said, worried. "Can't he find a key and get in?"

"I'll suggest that," he promised. He forced a smile. "Go graduate. You've worked hard for this."

She smiled. "Yes, I have. Now all I have to do is decide if I want to go on to graduate school or get a job."

"A job?" he scoffed. "As if you'll ever need to work."

"You're rich," she pointed out. "I'm not."

"You're rich, too," he argued. He bent and kissed her cheek, a little uncomfortably. He wasn't a demonstrative man. "I'm so proud of you, honey."

"Thanks, Daddy!"

"Don't forget to turn the tassel to the other side when the president hands you your diploma."

"I won't forget."

THE CEREMONY WAS LONG, and the speaker was tedious. By the time he finished, the audience was restless, and Niki just wanted it over with.

She was third in line to get her diploma. She thanked the dean, whipped her tassel to the other side as she walked offstage and grinned to herself, imagining her father's pleased expression.

It took a long time for all the graduates to get through the line, but at last it was over, and Niki was outside with her father, congratulating classmates and working her way to the parking lot.

She noted that, when they were inside the car, her father was frowning.

"I turned my tassel," she reminded him.

He sighed. "Sorry, honey. I was thinking about Blair."

Her heart jumped. "Did you call Jameson?"

"Yes. He finally admitted that Blair hasn't been sober for three days. Apparently, the divorce is final, and Blair found out some unsavory things about his wife."

"Oh, dear." She tried not to feel pleasure that Blair was free. He'd said often enough that he thought of Niki as a child. "What sort of things?"

"I can't tell you, honey. It's very private stuff."

She drew in a long breath. "We should go get him and bring him to the ranch," she said firmly. "He shouldn't be on his own in that sort of mood."

He smiled softly. "You know, I was just thinking the

same thing. Call Dave and have them get the Learjet over here. You can come with me if you like."

"Thanks."

He shrugged. "I might need the help," he mused. "Blair gets a little dangerous when he drinks, but he'd never hit a woman," he added.

She nodded. "Okay."

BLAIR DIDN'T RESPOND to her father's voice asking him to open the door. Muffled curses came through the wood, along with sounds of a big body bumping furniture.

"Let me try," Niki said softly. She rapped on the door. "Blair?" she called.

There was silence, followed by the sound of footsteps coming closer. "Niki?" came a deep, slurred voice.

"Yes, it's me."

He unlocked the door and opened it. He looked terrible. His face was flushed from too much alcohol. His black, wavy hair was ruffled. His blue shirt, unbuttoned and untucked, looking as if he'd slept in it. So did his black pants. He was a little unsteady on his feet. His eyes roved over Niki's face with warm affection.

She reached out and caught his big hand in both of hers. "You're coming home with us," she said gently. "Come on, now."

"Okay," he said, without a single protest.

Jameson, standing to one side, out of sight, sighed with relief. He grinned at her father.

Blair drew in a long breath. "I'm pretty drunk."

"That's okay," Niki said, still holding tight to his hand. "We won't let you drive."

He burst out laughing. "Damned little brat," he muttered.

She grinned at him.

"You dressed up to come visit me?" he asked, looking from her to her father.

"It was my graduation today," Niki said.

Blair grimaced. "Damn! I meant to come. I really did. I even got you a present." He patted his pockets. "Oh, hell, it's in my desk. Just a minute."

He managed to stagger over to the desk without falling. He dredged out a small wrapped gift. "But you can't open it until I'm sober," he said, putting it in her hands.

"Oh. Well, okay," she said. She cocked her head. "Are you planning to have to run me down when I open it, then?"

His eyes twinkled. "Who knows?"

"We'd better go before he changes his mind," her father said blithely.

"I won't," Blair promised. "There's too damned much available liquor here. You only keep cognac and Scotch whiskey," he reminded his friend.

"I've had Edna hide the bottles, though," her father assured him.

"I've had enough anyway."

"Yes, you have. Come on," Niki said, grabbing Blair's big hand in hers.

He followed her like a lamb, not even complaining at her assertiveness. He didn't notice that Todd and Jameson were both smiling with pure amusement.

WHEN THEY GOT back to Catelow, and the Ashton ranch, Niki led Blair up to the guest room and set him down on the big bed.

"Sleep," she said, "is the best thing for you."

He drew in a ragged breath. "I haven't slept for days," he confessed. "I'm so tired, Niki."

She smoothed back his thick, cool black hair. "You'll get past this," she said with a wisdom far beyond her years. "It only needs time. It's fresh, like a raw wound. You have to heal until it stops hurting so much."

He was enjoying her soft hand in his hair. Too much. He let out a long sigh. "Some days I feel my age."

"You think you're old?" she chided. "We've got a cowhand, Mike, who just turned seventy. Know what he did yesterday? He learned to ride a bicycle."

His eyebrows arched. "Are you making a point?"

"Yes. Age is only in the mind."

He smiled sardonically. "My mind is old, too."

"I'm sorry you couldn't have had children," she lied and felt guilty that she was glad about it. "Sometimes they make a marriage work."

"Sometimes they end it," he retorted.

"Fifty-fifty chance."

"Elise would never have risked her figure to have a child," he said coldly. "She even said so." He grimaced. "We had a hell of a fight after the Christmas I spent here. It disgusted me that she'd go to some party with her friends and not even bother to call to see how I was. She actually said to me the money was nice. It was a pity I came with it."

"I'm so sorry," she said with genuine sympathy. "I can't imagine the sort of woman who'd marry a man for what he had. I couldn't do that, even if I was dirt-poor."

He looked up into soft, pretty gray eyes. "No," he agreed. "You're the sort who'd get down in the mud with your husband and do anything you had to do to help him.

Rare, Niki. Like that hothouse orchid pin I gave you for Christmas."

She smiled. "I wear it all the time. It's so beautiful."

"Like you."

She made a face. "I'm not beautiful."

"What's inside you is," he replied, and he wasn't kidding.

She flushed a little. "Thanks."

He drew in a breath and shuddered. "Oh, God…" He shot out of the bed, heading toward the bathroom. He barely made it to the toilet in time. He lost his breakfast and about a fifth of bourbon.

When he finished, his stomach hurt. And there was Niki, with a wet washcloth. She bathed his face, helped him to the sink to wash out his mouth then helped him back to bed.

He couldn't help remembering his mother, his sweet French mother, who'd sacrificed so much for him, who'd cared for him, loved him. It hurt him to remember her. He'd thought Elise resembled her. But it was this young woman, this angel, who was like her.

"Thanks," he managed to croak out.

"You'll be all right," she said. "But just in case, I'm going downstairs right now to hide all the liquor."

There was a lilt in her voice. He lifted the wet cloth he'd put over his eyes and peered up through a growing massive headache. She was smiling. It was like the sun coming out.

"Better hide it good," he teased.

She grinned. "Can I get you anything before I leave?"

"No, honey. I'll be fine."

Honey. Her whole body rippled as he said the word. She tried to hide her reaction to it, but she didn't have the experience for such subterfuge. He saw it and worried. He couldn't afford to let her get too attached to him. He was too old for her. Nothing would change that.

She got up, moving toward the door.

"Niki," he called softly.

She turned.

"Thanks," he said huskily.

She only smiled, before she went out and closed the door behind her.

*Don't miss*
*WYOMING RUGGED by Diana Palmer,*
*available December 2015 wherever*
*Harlequin® HQN books and ebooks are sold.*
*www.Harlequin.com*

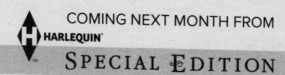
### #2449 Fortune's Secret Heir
*The Fortunes of Texas: All Fortune's Children*
by Allison Leigh

The last thing Ella Thomas expects when she's hired to work a fancy party is to meet Prince Charming...yet that's what she finds in millionaire businessman Ben Robinson. But can the sexy tech mogul open up his heart to find his very own Cinderella?

### #2450 Having the Cowboy's Baby
*Brighton Valley Cowboys*
by Judy Duarte

Country singer Carly Rayburn wants to focus on her promising singing career—so she reluctantly cuts off her affair with sexy cowboy Ian McAllister. But when she discovers she's pregnant with his child, she finds so much more in the arms of the rugged rancher.

### #2451 The Widow's Bachelor Bargain
*The Bachelors of Blackwater Lake*
by Teresa Southwick

When real estate developer Sloan Holden meets beautiful widow Maggie Potter, he does his best to resist his attraction to the single mom. But a family might just be in store for this Blackwater Lake trio...one that only Sloan, Maggie and her daughter can build together!

### #2452 Abby, Get Your Groom!
*The Camdens of Colorado*
by Victoria Pade

Dylan Camden hires Abby Crane to style his sister for her wedding...but his motives aren't pure. To make amends for the Camden clan's past wrongdoings, Dylan must make Abby aware of her past. But what's a bachelor to do when he falls for the very girl he's supposed to help?

### #2453 Three Reasons to Wed
*The Cedar River Cowboys*
by Helen Lacey

Widower Grady Parker isn't looking to replace the wife he's loved and lost. Marissa Ellis is hardly looking for love herself—let alone with the handsome husband of her late best friend. But fate and Grady's three little girls have other ideas!

### #2454 A Marine for His Mom
*Sugar Falls, Idaho*
by Christy Jeffries

When single mom Maxine Walker's young son launches a military pen pal project, she's just glad her child has a male role model in his life. But nobody expected Gunnery Sergeant Matthew Cooper to steal the hearts of everyone in the small town of Sugar Falls, Idaho—especially Maxine's!

---

**YOU CAN FIND MORE INFORMATION ON UPCOMING HARLEQUIN® TITLES, FREE EXCERPTS AND MORE AT WWW.HARLEQUIN.COM.**

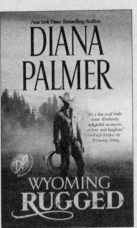

*New York Times* Bestselling Author

# DIANA PALMER

"It's a fast read with many absolutely delightful moments of love and laughter."
—*Fresh Fiction* on *Wyoming Strong*

## WYOMING RUGGED

$7.99 U.S./$9.99 CAN.

**EXCLUSIVE**
**Limited time offer!**

## $1.00 OFF

*New York Times* bestselling author
## DIANA PALMER

brings you back to Wyoming with a tale
of love born in Big Sky Country...

# WYOMING RUGGED

*Available November 24, 2015.*

*Pick up your copy today!*

**HQN**™

---

## $1.00 OFF the purchase price of WYOMING RUGGED by Diana Palmer.

Offer valid from November 24, 2015, to December 31, 2015.
Redeemable at participating retail outlets. Not redeemable at Barnes & Noble.
Limit one coupon per purchase. Valid in the U.S.A. and Canada only.

SPECIAL EXCERPT FROM

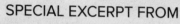

# SPECIAL EDITION

*When tycoon Ben Robinson enlists temp Ella Thomas
to help him uncover Fortune family secrets, will the
closed-off Prince Charming be able to resist the charms
of his beautiful Cinderella?*

*Read on for a sneak preview of
FORTUNE'S SECRET HEIR, the first installment in the
2016 Fortunes of Texas twentieth anniversary continuity,*
***ALL FORTUNE'S CHILDREN**.*

Ben figured it was only a matter of time before the security
guards came to check that he'd exited. But having gotten
what he'd come for, he had no reason to stay.

He went out the door and it closed automatically behind
him. When he tested it out of curiosity, it was locked.

"Crazy old bat," he muttered under his breath.

But he didn't really believe it.

Kate Fortune was many things. Of that he was certain.
But crazy wasn't one of them.

He looked around, getting his bearings before setting
off to his left. It was dark, only a few lights situated here
and there to show off some landscape feature. But he soon
made his way around the side of the enormous house and
to the front, which was not just well lit, but magnificently
so. He stopped at the valet and handed over his ticket to a
skinny kid in a black shirt and trousers.

He tried to imagine Ella dashing off the way this kid
was to retrieve his car, parked somewhere on the vast
property. He couldn't quite picture it.

But in his head, he could picture *her* quite clearly.

Not the red hair. That just reminded him of Stephanie. But the faint gap in her toothy smile and the clear light shining from her pretty eyes.

That was all Ella.

A moment later, when the valet returned with his Porsche, Ben got in and drove away.

*Don't miss*
*FORTUNE'S SECRET HEIR*
*by* New York Times *bestselling author Allison Leigh,*
*available January 2016 wherever*
*Harlequin® Special Edition books and ebooks are sold.*

www.Harlequin.com

# REQUEST YOUR FREE BOOKS!
## 2 FREE NOVELS PLUS 2 FREE GIFTS!

**H HARLEQUIN®**

# SPECIAL EDITION

## Life, Love & Family

**YES!** Please send me 2 FREE Harlequin® Special Edition novels and my 2 FREE gifts (gifts are worth about $10). After receiving them, if I don't wish to receive any more books, I can return the shipping statement marked "cancel." If I don't cancel, I will receive 6 brand-new novels every month and be billed just $4.74 per book in the U.S. or $5.49 per book in Canada. That's a savings of at least 12% off the cover price! It's quite a bargain! Shipping and handling is just 50¢ per book in the U.S. and 75¢ per book in Canada.* I understand that accepting the 2 free books and gifts places me under no obligation to buy anything. I can always return a shipment and cancel at any time. Even if I never buy another book, the two free books and gifts are mine to keep forever.

235/335 HDN GH3Z

Name _____ (PLEASE PRINT) _____

Address _____ Apt. #

City _____ State/Prov. _____ Zip/Postal Code

Signature (if under 18, a parent or guardian must sign)

### Mail to the **Reader Service:**
**IN U.S.A.:** P.O. Box 1867, Buffalo, NY 14240-1867
**IN CANADA:** P.O. Box 609, Fort Erie, Ontario L2A 5X3

**Want to try two free books from another line?**
**Call 1-800-873-8635 or visit www.ReaderService.com.**

* Terms and prices subject to change without notice. Prices do not include applicable taxes. Sales tax applicable in N.Y. Canadian residents will be charged applicable taxes. Offer not valid in Quebec. This offer is limited to one order per household. Not valid for current subscribers to Harlequin Special Edition books. All orders subject to credit approval. Credit or debit balances in a customer's account(s) may be offset by any other outstanding balance owed by or to the customer. Please allow 4 to 6 weeks for delivery. Offer available while quantities last.

**Your Privacy**—The Reader Service is committed to protecting your privacy. Our Privacy Policy is available online at www.ReaderService.com or upon request from the Reader Service.

We make a portion of our mailing list available to reputable third parties that offer products we believe may interest you. If you prefer that we not exchange your name with third parties, or if you wish to clarify or modify your communication preferences, please visit us at www.ReaderService.com/consumerchoice or write to us at Reader Service Preference Service, P.O. Box 9062, Buffalo, NY 14240-9062. Include your complete name and address.

HSE15